LITTLE MISS KICK-ASS
#1

Cosplay

FELICITY KATES

Cosplay

LITTLE MISS KICK ASS #1

is a reissue of
STEAM BUNNY/MY DESIRE
By Felicity Kates

First edition (Steam Bunny). August 14, 2014
Second Edition (My Desire) February 2016
Third edition (Cosplay) January 2020

Written by Felicity Kates.
Edited by Piper Denna.
Cover art and design by Kate Reedwood.
All rights reserved.

kcbooks@legacyhunter.space

ISBN-13: 978-1-7771102-0-8

Dedication

For Shannon.

.

Contents

Acknowledgments

To Shannon and all my reading friends at the **Kates Korner Fan Page and the Legacy Hunter Guild**—thank you! Without you and your love of reading, this book would never have reached 'The End' or have found a place in the world.

To Zara, writing goddess and inspiration, Piper, editor extraordinaire, and Nicole, my P.A., without whom I would be a disorganized mess. Thank you for your help and encouragement.

To Chris, my writing partner, business partner, and best friend. Thank you for keeping me sane and sticking with me despite the challenges life tosses our way. We got this!

To my husband, Mike, my son, Alex and all my wonderful friends and family cheering me on behind the scenes. I would be lost without each of you and your belief in me. Thank you.

And thank you, dear reader, from the bottom of my heart. I couldn't do this without you.

 Felicity

THE GLOVES ALWAYS went on last.

Cool satin, sliding over my fingers and up past my elbow like a decadent lick of chocolate against my creamy skin. A perfect fit of elegance for the extravagant costume I wore. Or so I was told. Usually. Unless my boss was in one of his moods, which I bet he'd be today. These weekend-long entertainment expos often made him snarly and this one had all the hallmarks of being super snarl-worthy.

With a contract on the line, including the chance at a TV deal, he needed me at my best to impress the Powers That Be. But did I want to stick out my neck—or rather my breasts—for the sake of helping an egotistical jerk score the deal of his lifetime? I used to think I did. I used to think we loved each other. But now I wasn't so sure. This was, after all, my last weekend working for him.

"You've gained weight," he said, his deep voice coarse with impatience. "The top's too tight."

Right. I deducted another point off my shrinking mental tally under 'Reasons I Should Stay,' and resisted the urge to laugh. Lucas Haskell was nothing if not predictable. With a tug, I finished adjusting the gloves and looked up, finding his reflection in the mirror opposite me where he lounged against the hotel room wall, arms crossed, watching each detail of my dressing with intense, ice-blue eyes.

With their thick fringe of dark lashes and the way they seemed to look right into my soul and read my heart's desire, I could get lost in those eyes. I had, in fact, done so many times, Lucas being the type of man a woman could never ignore once he'd entered her life, no matter how hard she might try to resist.

So why resist?

That's what I'd thought when we'd first met over a year ago. Ha! Stupid me. I should have known by the way my heart raced at his intent look as I'd walked in through his studio door. It wasn't attraction. It was my body telling me to run for the hills.

"Too tight? Really?" I asked sweetly and pursed my red-stained lips, turning to face him. The low-cut bodice did fit a lot more snugly across my breasts than when I'd had it measured last month. Craziness, since I'd lost an inch from my waist, a fact my best-friend-forever, Astrid Bitten, had fussed over as she'd helped me cinch up the corset this morning. But honestly, a costume like this went way beyond being too tight. Rabbit ears, lace and skin-hugging leather? I was dressed like a teenage boy's wet dream. "I like the way the new corset pushes my breasts up. You wanted more skin to show, didn't you?"

Leaning forward slightly, I perched against the countertop and let the vest-style corset do its work. The demi-cups of leather lifted my breasts, thrusting them outward for him to admire.

"Not that much," he muttered but his eyes widened ever-so-slightly in a satisfying flash of interest, which even his steel will couldn't hide, as I patted the generous amount of flesh cresting the top of my faux-fur bodice.

Yeah. Take that, buddy. Not yours. Not anymore. Stupid prick.

After all the time we'd worked so closely together, he should have figured out that ultimatums never, ever worked with me. And asking me three weeks ago to commit or leave? Dumb. Dumb, dumb, dumb. I held all the cards, right here in my hands.

His jaw flexed, nostrils flaring as I gave my breasts a little squeeze.

Fortunately, my mother's genes hadn't failed me

in the rack department (or my hips and thighs, unfortunately). Lucas had hired me for my curvy figure as well as my marketing skills. He enjoyed watching me, I knew. Enjoyed seeing me dressed up as Steam Bunny, his beloved comic book creation, brass gears, bunny ears and all.

It wasn't Lucas the throngs of hormone-jacked geeks came to see at these fan-boy comic conventions; it was me, Casey Jackson, aka Steam Bunny. Sure, they wanted his autograph, a signed copy of his latest book, but I drew the crowd with my silky bunny-in-heat act, and he knew it. The fact he now had second thoughts when seeing how much of me showed today, made me want to both slap and kiss him. He still cared, the territorial jerk, but did I?

What did I need him for?

A steady paycheck? Although he paid me well for the work I did as his assistant, I could work in almost any advertising agency in New York City making a whole bunch more. I knew how to work the social media scene. In fact, since word had gotten out about our imminent split, I'd had offers coming in to sign on at Grayson Advertising with Astrid and where Louboutins and Coach were the dress code instead of this skin tight, Victorian-style, slightly Goth, and definitely kinky, bunny suit.

So why stay?

Hot sex? Um, no. Well, maybe. Okay, so Lucas did have a gorgeously thick cock—and my lord, he knew how to use it—but I'd been doing just fine with my electric friend 'Thor' these past three weeks, thank you very much. Maybe it wasn't the same as feeling his strong hands on my body and experiencing that electricity I always felt when with him. But did I really need the excitement of being pleasured by the only man in the world I'd ever shared a mind-numbing orgasm with because I loved him with my entire being?

All right.

I'm a big enough girl to admit it. I stayed with Lucas Haskell because the idea of being without him left a hole in my heart I could hardly ignore. I'd been miserable these past three weeks, sick to my stomach, in fact. Barely eating, barely sleeping. A pathetic shadow of my normal self and it was all because of him.

The gorgeous, brilliant jerk.

When I'd applied to work as his marketing assistant, I'd expected to find a pudgy, basement dwelling, hygienically-challenged nerd so absorbed in his fantasy world he could barely utter a coherent word, let alone have an intelligent conversation. But at six-foot-four, with chiseled features capped by a shaggy mane of dark hair, Lucas looked just as good in the casual leather jacket and jeans he wore today as he did in a tux, his body kept in shape by a regime of push-ups and jogging.

Sometimes, like at two in the morning, the creative drive would hit him hard, charging up his astounding mind so he couldn't sleep, and if he couldn't draw it out on paper, he'd work it off, pounding the pavement, or skipping rope like a champion boxer, his breath coming fast and sweat running in rivulets down his tattooed chest, giving him that manly scent I always detected when he was near. Bergamot soap and *him*.

It filled the room now, turning my mouth dry as he examined me, his intent gaze sliding over every inch of my body as he looked for a stitch or whisker out of place. I shifted, waiting, a trail of goose bumps rising in the wake of his burning scrutiny. Sweet Jesus, I loved how he looked at me as if he could never get enough. His hungry stare travelled up my stiletto boots, paused on my naked thighs and then dipped between my legs to stroke the contours of my stretchy velveteen bottoms. My clit throbbed as if he had touched it, inspiring a fluttering of excitement in my belly. I pressed my thighs together, needing to move under such intimate scrutiny as warmth spread outward from my core, heating me from the roots of my hair to my curling toes.

His brows flicked, his eyes darkening as if he knew exactly what his probing stare did to me and enjoyed every minute of my arousal and discomfort.

I stroked my breasts again, teasing him. Or was it me? My nipples ached today. Probably because they missed his awesome massages. His hands could work magic on my body, but he seemed content in keeping them tightly curled about his biceps in angry defiance of pleasuring me.

Dickhead.

This separation was all his fault. Separate hotel rooms. Seriously? After the intimacy we'd shared for so many months? I wouldn't call his refusal insulting, but it certainly stung like hell. Which, of course, was the point.

His rejection was based on pride. Punishment. I could expect no less for turning down his proposal. The ring he'd offered three weeks ago had been beautiful, the look in his eyes profound. But I wanted a partnership, not a noose.

Unfortunately, he wanted a wife.

I'd tried to explain I was rejecting the

institution of marriage rather than him, but he hadn't wanted to listen, and I'd rather die than beg. Nope. If he wanted me back—and it seemed pretty clear by the tight bulge in his pants crotch that he still wanted me—he'd have to make the first move.

So, here we stood at an impasse. The few feet between us of the Chicago Marriott's finest broadloom carpet might as well have been the Grand Canyon.

Well, shit. What was it going to take to make him come over to my side? If I teased him some more, would he finally end this insane refusal to touch me? Maybe, just maybe, he'd do more than stare and critique today. Maybe he'd see reason and use some of the energy charging the air between us by working it off on me.

I slid my hands downward from my breasts, letting my fingers trail over the smooth leather and buckles of my corset, inching lower until I touched the lacy fringe of my velveteen bottoms. His eyes followed the movement, narrowing as my satin-covered fingers gently played with the delicate lace.

Was he daring me to go further? Ha!

Grinning, I slipped my fingers beneath my waistband, enjoying the tense stillness of his body as he concentrated on the naughty progress of my hands.

Idiot. Did he really think I'd give him the pleasure of a peep show? He got off on that kind of thing. So did I, but not today. Today he'd have to apologize for being such a prick, if he wanted me to play peek-a-boo and bring myself to orgasm for him. He might be the boss, but I was in charge here and enough was enough.

With a sultry chuckle, I slid my hands back out of my bottoms and planted them on my hips. "Well," I said, giving him a nonchalant shrug. "I'm ready to go downstairs to the conference if you are."

His sharp intake of breath was followed by a muttered obscenity that reached across the impasse and made my grin widen.

"What was that?" I asked, cupping my hand behind my ear in coy pretense of mishearing.

"Holy puck? Are you into worshipping hockey now?"

Leather creaked as he unfurled his arms, his black jacket sliding loose and easy as he pushed away from the wall. His imposing aura of manly yumminess seemed to fill the entire room as he straightened to his full height and speared me with 'The Look'.

Uh-oh.

The breath left my lungs at the sparking force of that look. Angry spots of color dotted his cheeks and for a moment the tiniest of doubts flashed in my mind. Maybe I'd misplayed this situation. Had I pushed him too far? What if he left instead of admitting he was wrong?

But he moved toward me, not away, his mouth curling up at the corners, exposing his pearly whites in a welcome, if somewhat predatory, smile.

Well ho-lee-shit. He hadn't intentionally approached me like this for weeks. Three very long weeks where I'd contemplated my empty bed each night. Hoping, praying we could just get past this stupid argument about who owned whom and move forward together.

'The Look' deepened as he sauntered closer, trapping me against the countertop at my back. Yowzah. How did guys do that, anyway? Put all their unspoken intentions into the narrowing of an eyelid and quirk of a brow? I wouldn't have minded except the unspoken intentions sparking from Lucas's eyes weren't just hot desire. Nope. These were more like frustration and murder and hot desire.

I'd hurt him by refusing his proposal. I knew that. I'd dented his magnificent pride, and God above how I wished I had not. But I wasn't cut out for marriage. It did things to people. Changed them and chained them. I didn't want that for either of us.

His warm scent tickled my senses as I breathed in deep, filling my mind with vivid thoughts of peeling off his jacket and the white t-shirt beneath, and tracing the swirling Celtic love knots tattooed across those magnificent pecs, now less than half a foot away from me.

I grasped the countertop instead. No way was I giving in here, no matter how much my pulse raced to be so near him again.

"Casey." His voice was warm velvet, caressing me with the sound of my name. His dangerous gaze swept over my face, trailing from my chin to the tips of my bunny ears, his eyes locking on mine.

"Yes?" I managed, despite the riot my brain had become at the mesmerizing intensity of those eyes.

He had me pressed against the hard edge of marble, his pelvis resting just above mine, but not quite touching. Nope, that was part of his game. The agonizing torture of being so near what I craved but could no longer have.

Well, he couldn't have me either. Not until he apologized. Stiffening my resolve not to cower under his onslaught of pheromones, I raised my chin, realizing too late that in doing so I exposed my throat to him as if asking for a kiss.

"You naughty girl," he whispered, and his smile widened, victory flashing across his features. "You still want me. Don't you, my little cock tease?"

I swallowed hard, unwilling to lie, yet unable to admit the shameful truth burning through my body and radiating from my skin. I did want him. I wanted every hard inch of him thrusting inside me as he called my name, declaring his love with his body and soul.

His fingers brushed at the long bunny whiskers glued to my cheeks, then whispered so close to the length of my neck the warmth of his hands prickled my skin. He skimmed my collarbone, down across my cleavage, and settled on the fake fur fringing my rack.

"Your breasts are so gorgeously plump. They're begging for me to touch them, aren't they, baby?"

Oh, God. My soul shook with the desire to give in and rip off my stupid restricting top. I needed him to ravish my aching flesh and bring us both to orgasmic bliss. But I bit my lower lip, hardly daring to breathe as he played there, primping the fabric into place, adjusting the lace frill of my too-tight bodice to his heart's desire, all the while sending waves of pleasure spiking to my lady parts as the fabric tugged my sensitive nipples and his heat brushed my skin.

Desire knotted my belly, hot and tight. He leaned in close to my neck and took a noticeable breath, inhaling what I knew to be his favorite perfume, vanilla spice. He'd given it to me for Christmas, not three months past. The memory of how we'd celebrated that night by giving each other gifts of intense pleasure made me break my vow not to moan.

The soft sigh escaped my lips as they parted in anticipation. My eyelids fluttered shut. He stood so close I could wrap my gloved arms around him and pull him closer still. I wanted to feel him against me, and he wanted to feel me too. Skin to skin, not just through clothes. I felt it in the heat of his hard body dwarfing mine, in the knotted cord of muscle as he braced one arm against the mirror behind me, bending down toward me, his lips brushing near my ear. So close, so very close. After all the long days of working separately over the past few weeks, awkward in the cold silence, in the distance between us, I trembled with the need to break this painful spell holding us apart.

"I'm going to give you something you need," he said, his sizzling breath teasing my skin, and his words my heart. "It fits right in here," he added, and in a surprise move, which abandoned the relative safety of my bodice and broke all of the rules of the game thus far, he plunged a long finger into the deep cleft between my tender breasts.

"*Oh*," I gasped, overcome by the exquisite feel of him sliding within my cleavage and parting my super-sensitized flesh in a not-very-subtle pantomime of his thick cock.

The sweet ache made my nipples tighten into almost painfully hard buds. Wetness instantly seeped between my legs. I imagined him suckling me, taking my nipples in his mouth and swirling them with his tongue. Playing with them while he made love to my breasts with his hands and then his cock. Stroking. Kneading. Thrusting long and hard. His hot spray coating my skin as we cried out together in passionate bliss. Oh God, yes. I'd missed that. I wanted that. Now.

I shifted toward him, encouraging him more. "Please," I whispered, no longer caring if it sounded like I begged.

"Are you ready, baby?" His finger moved slowly up and down, probing the hot depth of my cleavage.

"Yes…" *Sweet heaven above, yes!* I clutched the countertop for support and gritted my teeth against the growing urge to scream.

He chuckled, his hot breath tickling my ear. "Then here's your name card."

What?

My eyes flashed open.

A quick flick of his wrist tucked a plastic badge attached to a lanyard into the groove between my heaving breasts. And then he stepped back, laughter flashing in his eyes, blistering and triumphant.

For a moment I blinked in confusion. Then shock flared at the realization I'd been played. Gone were the delicious heat of his finger and the erotic spell he'd cast. In their place were cold hard plastic and sharp, sharp disappointment.

I stared in disbelief at the badge nestled snug in my cleavage, then back at him and his gloating smile. Give me something I needed? Jesus fucking Christ. And he accused me of being a tease? What a bastard. Nope, he was definitely not finished punishing me. Not by a long shot. But toying with my desire for him? That was a low blow.

"You are such an asshole." I snatched the card and tossed it onto the floor between us, spearing a hole in it with a satisfying stomp of my four-inch spiked heels.

"Am I?" He glared at me. "So, what was all this, then?" He cupped the air in front of his pecs and posed, mimicking the sexy way I'd squeezed my breasts at him, mocking me for mocking him.

A desperate act of a desperate woman, you idiot! The answer screamed in my head as my cheeks grew hot with the rush of humiliation thundering in my heart. Okay. So he had me there, but still, I'd just wanted to break through his thick skull and give us one last chance. A chance that seemed wasted now.

Nausea pinched my belly as I pushed away from the counter. But with anger strengthening my resolve, I glared up at him. "For weeks you won't touch me. You barely talk to me. You certainly won't listen to me." I poked him in the chest with a gloved finger. "Why can't we just deal with this and move forward?"

"We are moving forward. You left me. Remember?" He glared down his long, straight nose at me, shoulders rigid with anger. Unbending and undaunted.

I planted my hands on my hips. "As I recall, you threw me out."

"No. You quit."

"Yes, I quit," I said, exasperated. "You'd told me to leave if I couldn't agree to your terms. What was I supposed to do?"

"You were supposed to marry me," he

whispered.

And there it was, plain as all hell in his eyes and voice, in the way he held himself so rigid, yet so completely vulnerable. The anguish and pain of my rejection as new today as three weeks ago when I'd speared him through the heart with my cruelly whispered, *"No."*

I suspected he'd not slept much since then, or drawn, or been able to eat. Like me, he was living a half-life of loneliness, the shadow of which left dark circles under his gorgeous eyes and made his pale skin tight.

It killed me to see him this way, to know I had done this.

I loved everything about Lucas. (Or at least I had until now.) From the sexy stubble on his jaw to the way he smiled when deep in thought, his mind bursting with ideas as he sketched them onto paper, sharing with me his excitement in the art we brought to life.

That was the thing I'd lost the most, the thing I missed each second of each day. Yes, Lucas was attractive and a hell of a lover, but all of that came from inside him, in the way he looked at the world, letting his imagination flow through the pen in his hands. When we shared our ideas while sitting on the floor of his studio, pens and papers scattered about while we ate shawarma and sketched our dreams—we were linked, he and I, and good together, so good it seemed like magic.

Except now that magic was warped and twisted, a broken thing I didn't know how to fix.

If he'd asked for just commitment, I would throw myself into his arms and never leave. In my heart of hearts, I was already there. But I couldn't marry him. I just couldn't. I'd seen too many friends end up living like zombies that way, their souls sucked dry as they lost themselves to the ritual of being Mr. and Mrs.

Marriage was called an 'Institution' for more than one reason. I mean, just look at my mother. Broken by divorce, the bitterest person I knew. She'd lost interest in everything around her once my father left. A once-promising art career with shows at galleries in Manhattan and L.A., thrown away for what? A marriage that she'd given everything to and it'd busted up anyway. She hadn't picked up a paintbrush in years. I didn't want that to happen to Lucas and me. I loved him too much. I loved *me* too much. And he wanted me to give him an answer I didn't have it in me to give.

He saw it in my eyes even before I parted my lips to speak, his expression turning hard and cold.

He shook his head in disgust, cutting off my "I can't—" with an angry twist of his lips.

"Save it, Casey." He clawed a hand through his hair, the dark, silky strands slipping through his fingers and falling back into the shaggy mane I adored. "The signing starts in five. Just meet me downstairs and don't be late. You *can* do that, can't you?"

He didn't wait for my reply, just turned and left my hotel room. I flinched with the force of the slammed door, the sharp crack echoing the breaking of my heart.

My last convention as Steam Bunny.

My choice.

But what about that happenstance lurking in the background? That wildcard nagging at the back of my mind, offering a different explanation for my sore breasts and persistent nausea? That soft little whisper which grew stronger every day asking, *"What if your period's not just a bit late?"*

Yeah. What about that?

Lucas and I were in this together for business, or so I had thought. Except now he hated the ground I walked on, proving my point that marriage, even the thought of it, always ruined everything. A maybe-baby wouldn't change that.

I mentally crumpled up my list of 'Reasons I Should Stay' and tossed it in the trash as traitorous tears ran down my face, ruining my carefully applied bunny make-up and giving me raccoon eyes instead. I grabbed a Kleenex from the counter to staunch the messy flow.

Yeah. I had a problem. I loved Lucas Haskell, but I loved me too. So why did I have to choose between us?

"Fuck it," I said. Dropping the Kleenex, I gave up trying to fix the dark smears spreading around my green eyes and down my pale cheeks. I'd go as Goth Steam Bunny today. The world could see me looking like crap. I certainly felt like it. With a resolved sniffle, I smoothed my costume, tucked a loose strand of my strawberry blond curls about my ear, and straightened my spine.

Right. Lucas could go to hell for making me feel like shit. I had a job to do, fans to see and a contract to secure for my future whether Mr. Haskell was in it or not.

Rescuing the nametag still stuck to the heel of my shoe, I slung it around my neck, and on a vindictive whim, tugged down the bodice again, heightening the plumpness of my breasts and undoing all of Lucas's adjustments. He had no say over me anymore.

With a last glance in the mirror, I forced a smile.

It was show time.

FRIDAY AT THE Fanglorious Comic and Entertainment Expo in Chicago, Illinois, consisted of a ten a.m. welcome by the event organizers and the beginning of three days' worth of fun for sci-fi and fantasy enthusiasts, including How-to seminars, Q and A sessions, the chance to meet celebrities, a masquerade party, and, of course, shopping. Did I say shopping? I meant the mint-in-box-signed-event-exclusive-bargain-hunting otherwise known to the professional collector as Credit-Card Crack.

Wall-to-wall vendor booths packed the main

hall, peddling comic books, graphic novels, figurines, movies, toys, artwork, miniatures, posters, music, and costumes of every kind. Wanna be an elf? You could be an elf, or a superhero, or a *My Little Pony* character, or a *Star Wars* Jedi.

Whatever you wanted to dress up as, you could find it here. And then there were the accessories: weaponry (real and otherwise), techie gizmos and gadgetry, make-up, wigs, hats, jewelry, and unique hand crafted items, including some gorgeous custom-fitted shoes by my favorite burlesque shop, Little Miss Kick-Ass, which I'd absolutely *had* to order. Black stilettos with ribbons laced up the heel like a corset? No way could I leave those lovelies behind. Talk about sexy as all hell to wear, not to mention they'd be useful to cork Lucas in the head with if he didn't stop being an ass.

And maybe it was the growing interest in fan-based culture, but looking across the convention hall, jostling with excited fans snatching up memorabilia no matter what the cost, it occurred to me for the umpteenth time that the organizers should have picked a bigger venue, or added an extra day, or something. Because this was freakin' nuts.

"This is freakin' nuts," Astrid said, echoing my thoughts as we scanned the noisy crowd. She handed me a bottle of water off the table where we worked in the roped-off section assigned for celebrity autographs. "You'd think it was San Diego Comic-Con or something."

I nodded wholehearted agreement as I perched my butt on the table and took a long sip, grateful for the excuse to sit. This convention wasn't the biggest of the year scheduled for mainland USA, but you'd never have known it. An hour and a half into the two-hour autograph and photo-op session for Lucas and I, and the line of fans had yet to let up. In fact, it just seemed to get longer.

Realizing the demand, we'd agreed to add another hour, not wanting to turn anyone away, but I shook my head at the craziness of it all. We were nowhere near the ranks of celebrity status such as *Star Trek's* Shatner and Marvel Comics great Stan

Lee, yet we still commanded a certain buzz amongst the crowds. Or rather, a lot of buzz, judging by the size of things today. Good that business was growing, but still…ouch. I needed a break.

The stiletto boots had taken their toll, making my ankles throb and my toes numb. But worse than that, Lucas had been right. The new bodice really was too tight, and my breasts ached, screaming to be free of the confinement.

"You still feel sick?" Astrid asked, peering up at me from her chair at the table. She'd traded in her designer outfits for jeans and a *Steam Bunny* t-shirt to volunteer her expertise with Photoshop for the weekend, acting as our camera tech and printing the glossy 8x10's she took of us and the fans. Lucas would have hired out for help, but Astrid had insisted. No way in hell, she'd said, would she let me go through this break-up with 'that-fucking-bastard-prick-who-doesn't-know-what-he's-losing,' aka Lucas, alone.

I nodded, taking another sip of water and hoping it would stay down. Her lips pressed into a line, her eyes narrowing in a knowing look, which I deftly skirted. In typical Astrid fashion, she'd helped me fix my tear-streaked make-up, while whacking me over the head with her suspicions, forcing me to face that nagging wildcard. Sore breasts, nausea, Aunty Flow being late for her monthly visit… yeah, okay, it's not as if it hadn't crossed my mind before.

Either I was about to have a period from hell, or birth control pills sucked and Lucas had knocked me up. But as it only cemented the fact that he was a jerk, I didn't want to think about it right now. It was just nerves screwing with my hormones anyway. It had to be. Otherwise Karma was the biggest bitch ever.

"God, Casey. This is absolute bullshit," Astrid snapped, yelling in my ear to be sure I'd heard her over the din. The noise level in the hall rivalled a packed bar on a Saturday night. "That bastard should be taking care of you, not working you to death and making you cry."

"I'm not doing it for him," I yelled back with a quick glance at the bastard in question, sitting nearby, seeming oblivious to our conversation while signing the cover of his latest graphic novel.

From the way he smiled and chatted comfortably with the fans while he scrawled his signature for them, you'd never know Lucas had a morbid fear of crowds. He preferred his privacy to being the life of a party, but I'd convinced him right from the get-go to give the convention circuit a try. He needed to get out there and meet people in person if he wanted to connect with his market. And a guy with looks like his? Well, he was sure to draw attention. Unfortunately, it'd never occurred to me at the time what kind of attention that might be.

A growing crowd of giggling girls followed him around at conventions these days, flirting and asking for his autograph. But not on their copy of his latest book. Oh no, that would be too normal. They wanted his imprint on their skin. Legs, arms, butts and bellies (pregnant or otherwise), anything was fair game (minus nipples and naughty parts). And as they paid for the privilege, who was Lucas Haskell to disappoint an adoring fan?

The pretty-young-thing in front of him leaned across the table, the bodice of her Steam Bunny costume pulled so low he could probably see her religion. He dutifully followed her finger, taking a good long look at what she offered as she pointed to a spot on her breast, just above the edge of her quite-visible bra cup where she wanted him to write his name.

Yep. No wonder he was smiling.

Maybe he'd get congested balls and die.

"What a dickhead," Astrid muttered.

"It's just business," I said with a shrug, ignoring my desire to slap the smile off the dickhead's face. "Besides, I'm not doing this for him," I repeated. "I'm doing it for them." And I nodded toward the sea of people waiting to meet me.

Lucas? Yeah. I could go without ever seeing his smarmy face again. Probably. Maybe.

But the fans? I loved these people who'd embraced me as Steam Bunny with open arms, sharing with me their need to step out of reality and dress as something different for a day while I did the same. I fed off the energy and noise of the crowd, enjoyed the scents of cheap pizza and too-sweet soda wafting through the air like at a summer carnival. Well, normally I did, but today I was distracted by my aching feet, my aching back and my aching heart. I would miss this job, Lucas be damned.

"Right." Astrid rolled her big blue eyes. "Like this could ever be fun. These people are terminally weird. I mean, look at this guy…" Her fingers flew over the keyboard as she quickly chose the best shot of three and adjusted the lighting. "Even I know Tron did not have a neckbeard, or a pot belly. That's just lovely, by the way. A stretchy white spandex body suit? He has bigger breasts than me. And…" She peered at the screen. "*O… M…G…* I can see his nipples!"

"Don't be such a biatch." I laughed. "He's just having some fun." And he'd been all right to take a picture with. Hover-hands instead of the ass-grabber type.

She wrinkled her nose. "Well, he's never going

to get laid dressed like that."

"You'd be surprised what people like."

"Eew, gross." She waved her manicured nails in the air and made a sour face. "Don't even go there. Totally TMI. There." She tweaked a few pixels with her digital brush. "His nips are gone, but I can't do anything about his package. Do you think that's as big as it gets? Poor guy." She shook her head with such mournful sadness, I couldn't help laughing again.

I gave her shoulders a quick hug, knowing she played the diva role on purpose, trying to cheer me up.

Though Astrid would always be more comfortable shopping on Fifth Avenue than slumming it with the cos-player crowd, she'd do just about anything to make me smile. And for all the hoity-toity condescension she could dish out at times, she was an amazing person. Not only a talented designer, she was tall, blond and statuesque, a beauty who had one of those annoyingly fast metabolisms which allowed her to eat cheesecake without ever gaining a pound. I should probably have hated her for that, but our common love of chocolate, ice cream and sappy movies had gotten us through some of the worst moments of our lives.

Like when my dad had left when I was thirteen, leaving me alone, awkward, and in braces, to take care of my mother and her basket case of misery. Astrid had stayed with me while I cried that weekend, not judging, just listening as I explained my deepest fears that I was rotten inside and unlovable and my dad had left because of me.

And then years later, when she'd been pregnant at sixteen, and so completely frightened to tell her parents she'd screwed up. I'd held her hand while she'd trembled and cried, standing before them and fessing up her secret sin. Maybe it'd been the stress of their resentment and anger, or their disappointment that Astrid hadn't been a 'perfect girl'. But it hadn't mattered in the end that she'd told them the truth, because two weeks later the baby had died in an early term miscarriage, taking a piece of Astrid as well.

Raising her sculpted brow, she handed me the glossy print to sign as it slid from the printer. "Better watch this next one." She made a show of looking past me and winking. "She's got a pretty big gun."

"Are you really Th-team Bunny?" a tiny voice lisped. Dressed in a flowing white robe with her dark hair coiled into cinnamon-bun rolls on either side of her head, a mini Princess Leia from *Star Wars* strolled towards us, plastic Blaster swinging in its holster at her side.

I gave her my classic two-finger 'Bunny Salute' and a genuine smile as I stood. "The one and only," I said. Except that I wasn't, was I? Not anymore. Because Lucas would hire someone else and I would be replaced.

"Wath's-it like?" Mini-Leia asked, brown eyes gazing up at me with awe, her lips pulled wide in a gap-toothed grin. She must have been about seven or so, the age I'd been when I'd first seen *Return of the Jedi* on DVD and known what I wanted to be when I grew up. "Does your gun shoot real steam-powered bullets? Oh! Whath's wrong with your tail?"

The horror in her voice as she pointed at my behind made me want to laugh but I kept my expression serious as I answered her questions in sequence, "It's lots of fun. No, this gun isn't real, and…" Ignoring the bright spots of pain which flashed before my eyes, I bent down to her height and gave my ass a little shake. The fluffy tuft of faux-fur sewn to the back of my hi-cut bottoms dangled loosely where it jutted from between the slit in my ankle-length jacket. "Oh, dear." I pretended shock at the sight. "That's not very good, now is it?"

"Do you want a boo-boo bandage? I bet my mom-th's got one in her bag."

"Not to worry, your Highness," Lucas cut in, with a bow to Mini-Leia as he rose from his chair. "I'll take care of that for Ms. Bunny." He winked at me as he gestured at Astrid. "This one's a group shot, Ass-turd."

"No problem, Luke-Ass," she said sweetly and gave him a pissy look.

"You will?" I said, ignoring their silly nickname banter, my mind still stuck on the idea of Lucas taking care of my ass. And a wink? Seriously? Who was he kidding? The world grayed a little as I straightened, and blood rushed from my head.

He caught me by the arm and gave me a sharp, assessing look. "Definitely."

Wait. Was that real concern in his eyes or was he just playing it up for the crowd?

Mini-Leia grabbed his attention as she babbled excitedly at Lucas, my sorry tail forgotten, as with all women, as soon as he was in sight, her thoughts were now about him.

I didn't falter as he carefully steered me to the backdrop, just tottered a little in my stupid thigh-high boots, while I searched for some solid ground.

Click, click. Flash. Turn and smile. Wait while Astrid worked her magic with the glossy print. And all the while, Lucas kept his arm locked around me, surrounding me with the warmth of his body, that bergamot scent and his smile. Maybe it was all the female flesh being thrust in his face, but he seemed cozy toward me. Almost friendly, as if he'd forgotten all about this morning's argument. He was back to acting like my lover and rock. Just like the old times before I'd crushed his heart.

"You look like shit," he said, bending close to my ear, still smiling for the crowd as camera phones clicked.

"Wow. You seriously know how to flatter a girl." I glanced over my shoulder at my tail. "It's just a loose thread. I'll fix it tonight." *Ass-hole.* I knew his niceness was too good to be true, but that didn't stop my stupid heart from twinging anyway.

He shook his head, his gaze searching my face. "Let me guess. You didn't eat any lunch?"

Huh? "I wasn't hungry." I hadn't had any breakfast either, as I'd thrown it all up with this morning's bout of nerves, but that was beside the point.

"Casey." He dragged his fingers through his hair. "You are the stupidest smart person I've ever met.

Why didn't you tell me you weren't feeling well?" With a sigh, he called out, "Astrid?"

"Yes, Luke-Ass?"

"We're taking a quick break. I need to speak with Casey. Alone."

She looked at me as she handed over the print to sign. "You okay with that?"

I shrugged his warm arm off my shoulders, creating some distance again. I didn't need his manly shit confusing me, but I nodded at Astrid while I scrawled my signature across the print. Lucas added his own and gave Mini-Leia a parting smile that would have dazzled any woman in its path. She giggled, brandishing her picture like a trophy as she raced back to her dad.

"Okay, I can use a pee break anyway." Astrid glanced between us, looking unconvinced it was a good idea to leave me alone with him, and then waved her finger in warning at Lucas. "But if you make her cry again, I'll kick your ass. Casey isn't well."

"Yeah. I can see that. Come on." Grabbing my

hand, he pulled me away from Astrid and the crowd and towards the back wall as if I were a naughty child.

"Where are we going?" I tottered along in his wake, unable to do anything more than try to keep up with his long-legged pace. "All these people are waiting."

Ignoring me, he paused beside the exit and waved over a cute little convention volunteer with an Asian cast to her pixie-like features and a t-shirt that seemed a bit too snug. I'd noticed her earlier, hanging around the autograph booth, waiting to do his bidding. "Sorry for the delay." He gestured toward the waiting crowd. "But we'll be back in ten. Is there a quiet place we can eat?"

"Oh. Yes, Mr. Haskell. There's space in the hotel restaurant set aside for convention guests. If you'd like, I could get you something from the kitchen. Just let me know what you need, and I'll have it brought to you." She smiled at him, barely glancing at me, her cheeks squeezing out two sweet dimples for the world to adore. Too cute by far.

"I'd like a needle and thread if you can find one."

"Of course. I'll have it brought to your table." If she seemed surprised by that request, she didn't show it. But, uh-huh. I bet she would just love to take care of all of Lucas's needs by the way her gaze lingered on him as he nodded his thanks and yanked me into the hallway.

Silence surrounded us as the door closed, loud in the emptiness after the crushing noise from the convention hall. "Who's she?" I asked as we walked together down the plush corridor.

A soft smile played across his lips. "Some flower or something. Hyacinth."

"Of course." I forced a light laugh as my heart squeezed tight.

I was used to the flutter of feminine interest that surrounded Lucas wherever he went. I mean, a guy like him would always have women looking. But although he enjoyed the flirting, he'd never strayed from me since the day we'd met. Ever. Our relationship was built on trust. Yet it occurred to me now that for the past three weeks, our only contact had been business, and that while I had been pining for the pleasure of his company alone in my bed at night, perhaps Lucas had taken a different approach to relieving his frustration. He'd remembered her name with a little too much familiarity for a quick glance at her nametag.

He couldn't be seeing someone else already, could he?

The thought buzzed like a bee in my mind, pricking me with its stinger. It *would* explain the remarkable resilience he'd shown in keeping his libido in check to punish me.

Stupid jerk. And he said he still wanted to get married? Ha! Did he think I was that much of a fool? I was well aware that this 'caring-guy' act was just a glimpse of the old Lucas meant to tease me. On the other hand, the warmth of his solid grip through my satin glove did feel really good even if it was on temporary loan. I could play this game a bit longer.

He looked at me quizzically as we entered a

room in the restaurant filled with soft lights, linen-covered tables, and booths set into private alcoves. My stomach growled loudly at the scent of fresh brewed coffee, causing the patrons seated nearby to glance at us and smile as we made our way to a vacant booth.

Lucas grinned and gestured at the central buffet table laden with an assortment of finger foods and steaming silver warming trays. "What would you like?"

"Nothing," I whispered as a wave of nausea hit me. What was *that* smell? Tuna fish? Egg? It clung to the back of my nose, souring the desire for coffee. I sank onto the soft seat and rested my head on the cool tabletop, waiting for the sickness to pass. Thank God I was off my feet. No need to make a scene fainting. Or puking. Or both.

"Casey?" Lucas prompted, sitting down beside me.

"There is no Casey, only *Zuul*," I muttered, adapting my favorite line from *Ghostbusters*.

"Prickly-pear?" he coaxed, a smile in his voice.

He hadn't used that nickname in ages. I turned my face to see him.

"You have to eat something," he said softly.

My foolish heart leapt at the troubled look in his eyes as he played with my gloved fingers still loosely caught within his, a sweet gesture made all the more potent for its simple familiarity.

"You need to take care of yourself and keep your strength up," he added. "Lindstrom's here."

"What?" I asked, jerking upright and looking around. "Where? I thought he wasn't coming until tomorrow."

"Not *here*," Lucas said, shaking his head. "I mean he's here, at the convention."

"Oh." So that's what this was about. Race Lindstrom, the producer for L.A. based Ani-motion Inc. It was all business and the freakin' TV deal. Not about me at all. Definitely not 'us'. I pulled my hand from Lucas's grasp. "Don't worry," I said. "I know how to handle him."

His expression darkened. "That's what I want to talk to you about." He glanced around the room as if making certain Lindstrom hadn't magically appeared in the restaurant like a demon summoned by his name. "I've heard he's lurking, checking out the scene. Seeing who's hot and who's not with the fans, you know?"

Well, that could be good for the future of *Steam Bunny*, as we'd had an unprecedented turnout, but then there were all those rumors I was leaving. Which were true. Unless Lucas did something to change my mind, at the end of this convention I was *gone*. "Have you seen him yet?" I asked slyly.

"No."

I smiled. "Good. If he comes by the booth, I'll be sure to act extra nice."

His jaw tightened.

My phone chimed. I fished it out of my coat pocket and checked the incoming text:

Some Bat Guy just grabbed my ass.

I giggled, piquing Lucas's interest.

"Who's that?"

"Astrid."

"Incredible. It's been less than five minutes since

she's seen you. What the hell do you two talk about all the time?"

"Macramé," I said drolly. "Could you get me some Ginger Ale and saltines, please?"

He paused for a fraction of a second at the unusual request, his eyes darting to mine. "You're feeling that nauseous?"

I nodded and pasted on a smile.

He studied me in silence, and I could practically see the wheels turning as he rose and moved to the buffet table to do my bidding. *Yeah, just you wonder about that buddy.* He knew my monthly cycle and was good at math. Yep, I was over a week and a half late, and had been nauseous every morning for the past three days. Of course, he wouldn't know that since he'd been avoiding me. Separate hotel rooms did have some benefits. But I couldn't put this off forever.

I texted Astrid back: *Don't you mean Batman?*

Astrid: *No. Bat Guy. He's got a BG symbol on his chest and smaller ears.*

Me: *Oh, right. Is he cute?*

Astrid: *Mask. Cape. Lots of muscles. Interesting eyes.*

Ask him out. I typed, and then added: *Can U pick me up a baby test?*

I quickly turned my phone off to silence the flood of *OMG's!* I knew she'd be sending. I could face reality more easily without the sunshine chorus.

"I didn't know you liked Ginger Ale," Lucas said, sliding in beside me onto the seat again. He watched me carefully as he handed me the drink.

I took a hesitant sip through the straw. The sweet bubbles tasted wonderful. "I don't usually," I admitted with a grateful smile. "Thanks."

"But you do now." He opened the packet of soda crackers and handed one to me.

I popped it into my mouth and took a bite. "Looks like," I mumbled around the mouthful of dry crumbs. Yuck. Completely flavorless. How did people eat these things? I grabbed a napkin and spat them back out.

"But not the crackers."

"Not so much."

"What about some pickles and ice cream?"

My stomach roiled. I swallowed another swig of soda and choked it down with a sputter. Gasping, I put the drink on the table. Jesus, what a zinger. But he never had been stupid. "Can we not talk about food, please? And shouldn't we get going? There's a line of people waiting to see us."

He ignored my blatant attempt at escape and caught my fingers in his again. "Is there something important going on that you'd like to tell me about, Casey?"

Trapped between the seat, tabletop, and him, I had nowhere to run. I looked him straight in the eyes. "Depends on if you'd be willing to listen."

"I'm listening now."

Yeah, I bet you are. But I shook my head. "There isn't anything important going on, but I promise that if that changes, I'll let you know. Okay?" It wasn't an outright lie. Suspicions were not knowing. And I *would* tell him as soon as I knew for certain. In the meantime, there didn't seem to be any point in making a fuss about something that could very well be nothing. I'd been late with my period before.

He didn't seem to know what to make of that answer. His fingers played with the stubble gracing his chin as he considered whether I was hiding something or not, his devastating gaze piercing my heart.

"All right." He nodded after a moment. "I won't say I'm sorry for anything that's happened." And he gave my fingers a little squeeze. "But you know I'll always be there for you if you ever need me, don't you?"

"I know," I whispered.

Oh, damn. Damn, damn, damn, damn. I was about to get raccoon eyes again and I couldn't let him see that. Lucas was the kind of guy who would never leave a woman to raise a baby alone. Unlike my own father, he'd honor his obligations until his dying day. But it didn't change anything as far as I could see. A maybe-baby was the stupidest reason ever to get married. I knew how it felt to be an obligation. My existence had ripped my parents apart.

Hyacinth arrived with a sewing case. "Here you are, Mr. Haskell." She waited by the table, looking at him. "Can I get you anything else?"

"Yeah. Some more towels for my room, please, and a bottle of massage oil. Thanks." He flashed her one of his dazzling smiles and she blushed as she scurried away to take care of it for him.

Was that supposed to be for me, or her, or someone else entirely? His expression gave no hints as he focused on me again, but he watched me expectantly as if waiting for me to ask. No way was I playing that game. I was too tired, too sore and the idea of a sensual massage too cruel if meant for someone other than me.

"All right," he said with a decisive nod. "Take off your coat and come here." He patted the seat beside him. "Face the wall so I can see to your tail."

"What? We're doing this *now*?" I asked incredulously.

"Why not? I can sew."

"Yeah, I know, but…uh…" I took another sip of soothing soda, feeling a blush rise as my mind raced to figure out how to win this game when the rules kept changing. What was Lucas up to now?

The issue wasn't the sewing. I'd always been impressed with his ability to tack on a button and fix a tear. He cooked and cleaned up after himself too, unlike some guys. His mom had made sure her boy could take care of himself. Living as a single parent, she'd had to. Lucas had never known his dad, thanks to a drunk driver running a red on a cold winter's night, but he'd grown up knowing his limits. His one big vice was teasing the hell out of me. And taking off my ankle-length, cap-sleeved coat, well, I didn't have much on underneath. Just the corset over the tight bodice, hi-cut bottoms, lacy thigh-high stockings, and the boots. Without the coat acting as a skirt, the world—and especially him—would get a good view of my rather fleshy behind.

He raised a mocking brow as my silence stretched. "Feeling suddenly shy?"

"Yes."

He laughed. He knew full well I found the idea of people watching me in intimate situations exciting. But being so near him right now was honestly making me feel nervous. He knew exactly how to tempt me into losing control. And what would happen then?

Steaming hot jungle sex, that's what. With me losing this battle unless he said sorry for being a possessive dickhead first.

A husky giggle escaped me as pretense fell aside. This was a dangerous game we were playing. It was all or nothing, with our future at stake. And with his pulsing virility charging the current between us and that disarming look in his clear blue eyes, I literally ached to feel his strong hard body writhing against mine while he whispered in my ear, *"I love you."*

Goddamnit, I missed the closeness we'd shared.

But it was here, now, in the rich sound of his laughter and the way his smile reached his eyes. In the way he made me feel so excited and alive. It felt so *good* to have a glimpse of it back I could almost cry.

"Come on," he insisted, a devilish glint sparking his gaze. "It will only take a second."

Yeah. A second that would last an eternity while he slid his fingers beneath my bottoms and pressed his hand against my skin as he slipped that needle in and out, tacking my tail back into place. But if he was willing to put his anger aside and stop being cold and distant, then I would do whatever it took to not break this delicate spell.

Besides. Who was I to refuse a dare?

With a sultry smile, I slowly unbuckled my gun belt, shrugged out of my coat and did as instructed. Kneeling on the seat, I clutched the back, giving him a good look at my mostly naked ass.

The tail of Casey Rabbit

I SHOULD HAVE known better.

I mean, I *really* should have known better.

Kneeling there, showing my ass to the world, Lucas just inches away. What had I expected to happen? That he'd be a perfect gentleman? That he'd ignore my behind and just fix my tail while I knelt there in perfectly controlled detachment? Well, I can only assume the lack of food had made me so light headed I no longer thought clearly because A) Lucas had *never* been a perfect gentleman, and B) There was no way in heaven, hell or anywhere in between that I could ever be around him and remain perfectly detached.

Lucas was like Loki, the Norse god of mischief, and he'd apparently learned a thing or two from this morning's argument about how much I desperately wanted him. Instead of ignoring me into submission, he now seemed determined to drive me insane with desire. One slow, smooth caress at a time.

And holy hell, was it ever working!

His hands slid over the curves of my butt cheeks where they peeked from beneath the high cut of my stretchy velveteen bottoms, as if testing the firmness of my flesh had anything to do with my dangling tail. He gave it a little pull, and then caressed the plumpness of my behind again like he had all the time in the world.

It will only take a second, my, erm…ass!

"You're enjoying this, aren't you?" I asked, trying hard to keep my breathing steady. A new feeling spread outward from my belly, replacing the nausea with hunger, only it wasn't for food.

"Hell yeah," he chuckled, a throaty, pleasure-filled laugh which made the tiny hairs on the back of my neck prickle. "Aren't you?"

My turn to laugh. "Do I really need to answer that?"

There was only one real reason I'd ever agree to kneel on a restaurant seat in view of admiring strangers and allow him to explore my bum with his clever, knowing fingers. Deep down inside, I enjoyed it. Very, very much. Maybe it made me weak and maybe it meant I was a 'dirty girl,' as my mother loved to say, but I couldn't ignore the shiver of desire Lucas sparked within me. Every time he touched me, every stroke, every caress, a tingling zing of pleasure shot straight to my core.

"Absolutely gorgeous," he murmured, sliding his hands from the narrowness of my waist and over the generous flare of my hips. His fingers found the naked skin of my outer thighs and paused there, gently massaging the exposed flesh in tiny circles. "So soft," he whispered as if he missed that fact.

A wave of heat flashed across my body. *Oh God.*

I closed my eyes, fighting the urge to give in to the building desire to spread my legs wider and beg him to touch me inside. Foolish to get worked up over a compliment like that, but, damn, it was a relief to know this closeness was having an effect on him too.

He cleared his throat as his fingers left my thighs and moved upward again. "How did this happen anyway?" he asked. My tail wobbled as he wiggled it.

I opened my eyes and took a little peek backwards to find him fully engrossed in admiring my behind. Heh. How indeed? Maybe it'd come loose when he played me for a fool, wedged up against the edge of the marble countertop earlier? "Well," I hedged, facing the wall again with a smile. "Guys do like to grab it."

"Which guys?" he asked a little too fast.

My grin widened. "Um…pretty much all of them?" Actually, most of the fans respected our hands-off-the-bunny policy. It was the guy sitting behind me, driving me crazy with his gentle caressing massage, who seemed to have a problem knowing his place.

"I see," he murmured. "You should've complained to the management. Pretty shitty boss if he wouldn't care about something like that."

I shrugged, doing my best to tease him. "It's not important."

Oh, but what he was doing with his hands was, it seriously was. I bit my lower lip to stifle a moan as my thighs trembled from the sweep of his fingers brushing low across my ass cheeks. How far did he intend to take this? How far did I want it to go?

"Guys grabbing your ass isn't important?" A bite laced his tone, followed by a squeeze from his hands.

"It's just business," I said, being deliberately blasé, very glad he couldn't see the smile on my face. "Kind of an occupational hazard."

"And what would you call this?" He gave my bum a little stinging slap that sent unexpected ricochets of pleasure zinging through my lady parts. Shocked, I clutched the top edge of the seat and glared back at him.

"An invitation to kiss my ass." I growled, irritated by how close I was to orgasaming just from the stroking of his hands. This game was fun, but enough was enough. Anymore and I'd embarrass myself. "If you're going to fix my tail, then fix it. We need to sign some autographs. Remember?"

His brows rose. His tongue moistened his lips as they lifted at the corners. He knew exactly how he'd rattled me. Just like he knew exactly how to please me. And yeah, I'd always liked it when he played with my ass cheeks. His big, strong hands, cupping them, rubbing them, his teeth peeling off my panties and his lips trailing a deluge of soft, sexy kisses...I'd missed that. A lot.

But instead of putting his lips where his hands were, he let go of me and picked up the spindle of thread, snapping off a length with his long, ink-stained fingers. "As you wish," he said, a devilish sparkle in his ice blue eyes.

Okay. That was good, wasn't it? He'd stopped when I'd demanded. Things were under my control.

I took a deep breath. "You've been drawing again?" I asked, turning back to face the wall. A neutral subject would be good here before I flipped out.

"A bit," he acknowledged. "I had an idea for a new character. A nemesis for Steam Bunny."

"A new bad guy?" I asked intrigued.

"Yeah." He slipped his fingers beneath the edge of my bottoms and slid them across my bum, hiking up the thin fabric. The pull of the seam against my lady parts made me suck in a sharp breath, but other than a slight pause in his own breathing as he pinned my errant tail so he could sew it back into place, he seemed not to notice. "Hyacinth's been doing some posing for it," he added.

Hyacinth?

I stilled as the needle poked in, any pleasure from his touch lost as my stomach clenched and the nausea returned. He'd asked *her* to pose for him? Had it been in the nude like I used to do?

"Really?" I whispered, unable to keep my mouth sensibly shut. "When?"

"Last night."

"Ah." *Fuck. Fuck, fuck, fuck.* The thread pulled tight, the needle stabbing for another pass. I swallowed down the bile surging into my throat, but it was pretty damn close. A coughing fit shook me.

Lucas patted my back. He handed me my drink. "You okay?"

I took a long sip. "Yeah," I said as soon as I'd caught my breath and my stomach settled again. Putting the drink down on the table, I focused on the wall in front of me, avoiding his probing gaze. "She's very eager, isn't she?" *The little slut.* "Working late hours?"

"Very," he said with a hint of a smile in his voice. "She likes to be helpful."

"Oh, I bet," I acknowledged. "You've always been a big tipper."

The needle moved in and out as he resumed sewing, tugging the fabric against my behind as he re-pinned my tail, his deft fingers slipping back and forth across my skin like a snake hypnotizing its prey.

"I do find it interesting, though," I said as the silence built. "That if she's been assigned to assist *us*, she's spending all of her time with *you*."

"Probably because I'm the boss. You don't mind her helping me, do you?"

"Of course not. Why would I?" I lied, but try as I might, I couldn't keep the bitterness from my voice.

Jealousy. Frustration. They sat in my empty belly like a hard knot. A poor choice of meal on a very trying day. He was just playing with me. Teasing me. Teaching me a lesson. He'd picked up on my earlier suspicions and was using it against me now. I mean, Lucas was smart. He rarely missed a beat. But I couldn't help the voice of doubt whispering in my mind, '*What if he's really moved on?*'

I didn't want to care, but I did. I hated the thought of him being with anyone else. But I'd walked away, hadn't I? Turned down his proposal. I could expect to see him with girls like Hyacinth all the time now. No way would he wait around forever, playing silly games with me. And if I was pregnant? What then? *What then*?

"All done," he said and drew a final knot.

Looking down over my shoulder, I watched him put the needle onto the table, but his attention was on my body, his intent gaze moving slowly from my now perky tail and up my back. His fingers played with the strings of my corset, plucking them like a favorite guitar. "Who helped you tie this up?"

"Astrid." Who'd he think would be there to help me if not him? Oh! Oh, oh, oh! Was that a flicker of satisfaction deep in his eyes? Was he happy it hadn't been someone else?

The panic inside receded a little. Whether or not he'd begun seeing other women, he was still emotionally tied up with me. Ha! Time for a bit of jealousy tit-for-tat. Tease him a little in return. The dickhead. If he could throw Hyacinth in my face, I could do the same with the one man at this convention I knew without a doubt was interested in me, because he'd come all the way from L.A. to check me out. "Do you think Race Lindstrom likes leather or lace?" I asked with a careful note of contrived innocence. "I'm trying to plan what I should wear to the meeting tomorrow."

"It doesn't matter." He sounded slightly gruff. "You won't be going."

"What?" Stunned, I sat down on the seat with a thump, crushing my perky tail. "Why?"

Brow furrowing, he played with the needle on the table, spinning it in a circle. "He has a bad reputation."

I reached for my drink and took a sip. "You mean the one where he's rich, gorgeous, and loves to chase women? Or the one where he likes to screw people out of their rights when negotiating contracts?"

"Both."

Uh-huh. But we'd known that about Lindstrom before the convention and had planned to use his interest in me to help secure the deal. So, what had changed? Did Lucas think I'd sabotage it now that we were on the outs? That was downright insulting.

"Don't worry, Lucas," I snapped. "I can handle him. I won't fuck up your deal." Especially since it wasn't just his deal, it was mine too. I hadn't accepted any offers of employment from other agencies partly because I wanted to see what Lindstrom had to say about the future of *Steam Bunny*. I wanted the best deal possible for me and, okay I'll admit it, for Lucas too.

"I don't doubt your abilities to negotiate a good contract," he said, his words stiff with impatience. "I just don't want you prostituting yourself to get it."

"P-P-Prost—" I sputtered, incredulous. "Did you just say *prostituting*?" The room narrowed to include only him and his big, fat, mouth. "Is that what you think I do?"

He shook his head. "Casey—"

"Because I might remind you that this whole thing was *my* idea." I gestured at my costume. "*My* choice. And I don't do it for the money. I don't do it for you. I do it because it makes *me* feel good. It makes me feel sexy. So, if you think that makes me a whore, you can go fuck yourself." I tried to stand, ready to crawl over the table if necessary, to get away from him.

He caught me about the waist and shoved me onto the seat again, blocking my path with his big, hard body. "Calm down," he hissed in a low tone, his eyes flashing with anger. "I didn't mean you were a prostitute. It was a poor choice of words." He paused as his jaw clenched and unclenched, his gaze boring into mine. "You're the smartest, sexiest woman I've ever met. *Steam Bunny* would be nothing without you."

Oh. That was kinda nice. Was that his roundabout way of saying he wanted me to stay?

Some of the icy hurt inside me melted as a different kind of heat flared. That bergamot and hot manly-man scent of his rose from his skin, filling my head with dizzying thoughts of licking it off his flushed neck.

But still, where did he get off thinking he could tell me what to do after ignoring me for almost a month? "But you still don't want me negotiating with Lindstrom?" I asked.

"No."

I waited for him to elaborate.

He kept his lips pressed in a tight line.

"You don't own me, Lucas," I said, slowly, deliberately as I stared into his devastating eyes. "I love you, and I want to be with you. But. You. Don't. Own me." I pushed against his chest, punctuating each word with a shove, trying to build some space. I might as well have pushed against a brick wall.

Nostrils flaring, he sucked in a harsh breath. "Don't I?"

His hand tightened about my waist as he pulled me close, crushing me against him. Stunned, I stiffened as an instinctual part of me tried to protest his strength. But Lucas wasn't buying any of it. He held me captive as his head bent low. His fingers snaked into my hair to hold me steady as his lips possessed mine, silencing any protest I might make in a searing reminder of everything we'd ever been to each other.

He doesn't own you. My panicked brain tried to scream. *He will never own you.* But my body didn't care. It had been too long since he'd kissed me like this, and I couldn't control the rush of excitement pounding through my veins. My lips parted as his tongue pressed along the seam, allowing him access inside.

His taste—oh God, his taste! Mint and spice and him, a heady combination after so many weeks without. I moaned as he caressed my lips with his, our tongues sliding against each other as the pressure within me built. All the pent-up desire I'd held tightly reined pounded through me with the urgent need to be with him again.

I slid my gloved hands beneath his jacket and clutched at the t-shirt covering his sculpted chest, trying to get closer to the warmth of him. "Lucas," I breathed against the hot skin of his lips.

He pulled back a bit and looked deep into my eyes.

I'd been with other men, but no one had ever made me feel like Lucas. He completed me in every way. He was my equal. My deepest love. And if the hunger in his gaze was half of what he saw in mine, he'd know how much I wanted him. Right now.

"Jesus, Casey," he whispered, his fingers caressing my cheek. "Do you have any idea what you do to me?"

Not waiting for a reply, he pressed me back against the seat, heedless of my carefully arranged curls and the bunny ears perched on top. Pinned against his solid heat, he moved his lips over mine, branding me with his taste and overwhelming strength.

Swept along with the force of his desire, I let it wash through me, filling up all the empty spaces left so long neglected. His hands played over my body, caressing, stroking, squeezing, teasing my senses as his bergamot scent filled my mind. It felt so good— so *damn* good—to be kissed by him again, I never wanted it to stop.

I craved him, needed him. His hair slipped between my fingers as I wrapped a hand about the back of his neck, deepening the kiss. God in heaven, his heart beat just as madly as mine when his chest crushed my breasts. And I didn't care about the pain of my sensitive nipples trapped against that tight bodice and the solid wall of his body. Or the fact we were in a restaurant in view of anyone who cared to notice. I burned for Lucas Haskell and I wanted him inside me.

His cock felt thick and hard, straining against his jeans as I pressed my hand along the bulge. I remembered that length and how good it fit inside my body. Did he remember too? I found his tip and rubbed it through the denim, causing him to groan so deeply it rumbled through me straight to my core.

He moved his lips from mine, trailing kisses to my ear. "You are so fucking sexy," he breathed, the hunger in his tone turning me on even more. "I love the taste of your skin." He licked my neck and gave it a tiny nip, causing a shiver to ripple involuntarily down my spine. "You want me to fuck you, don't you, baby?" His hot breath whispered against my cheek. "You want me to make you scream?"

My fingers spasmed as they tugged at the fly of his jeans. *Oh, dear God in heaven. Yes!*

"Right here. Right now. In front of all these people," he continued in his velvet voice, curling my toes with the heat of it. "I know exactly how to make you come."

Okay. That was kinda embarrassing. Mostly because it was completely true. I burned for him, and he knew it, but after this morning's disappointment, was he teasing me again? I wasn't willing to take that chance. I needed reassurance.

"Prove it," I said, caressing his bulging crotch and holding his hot hungry gaze with mine.

He smiled, his teeth flashing like a wolf excited by the hunt.

His hand slipped from my hip, his fingers trailing a line of fire as they swept over my naked thigh. "Open for me," he demanded.

I did as instructed, widening my legs a bit more. He immediately dipped between them, brushing along the velveteen seam covering the cleft of my mound.

"Oh...fuck." I whispered as my folds throbbed, eager for more than just his touch.

I closed my eyes, leaning my head back against the seat as sensations ripped through me, making it hard to think, let alone catch my breath.

"Look at me, Casey," Lucas insisted. "If you don't keep looking at me, I'll stop."

My eyes popped open at his no-nonsense tone. There were rules to this game, and I knew he meant business. He liked to see me come. I lifted my head again and stared him straight in the eyes.

"Good girl," he murmured a satisfied gleam in his devastating gaze. He rewarded me by swirling a gentle "S" pattern over the seam of my crotch.

My breath caught, passing through my lips in an uneven gasp. I abandoned trying to undo his jeans and clutched the seat instead, hanging on for dear life as he steered me closer to orgasm.

It wouldn't be long. I'd been halfway there before we started this little game.

Trapped between the seat, wall, table and him, I had nowhere to run to and nowhere I'd rather be. The background murmur of the restaurant faded he stroked me lightly, slowly, his eyes locked onto mine, the intensity of his gaze deepening as I bit my lip to stifle the moan building inside.

I squirmed, wanting him to move his fingers faster, to put me over the edge right now, but he held back, enjoying the way he made the blood pound in my veins and my body quiver.

"Shit," I moaned. "You're such a teasing asshole, Lucas. This isn't funny anymore."

"Yes, it is." He laughed, a heavy sensual chortle. "And you love every minute of it, my naughty minx."

I managed an unintelligible growl in response as he swept his thumb over my clit again.

Because he did know me, knew exactly what I liked, exactly how much pressure to exert with each stroke of his fingers. I had no secrets from him when it came to my desires. We'd played this game many times before. Touching each other under a dinner table, or in a darkened movie theater, bringing each other to the brink of orgasm while pretending not to be aroused.

Except there was no pretending here. I

whimpered as he stroked me, so close to the edge I shivered.

"Jesus. You're so wet," he said softly, the hoarse need in his voice an instant aphrodisiac. And if I hadn't been excited before, I certainly was now as liquid seeped between my folds. My eyelids drooped shut as I shifted, squeezing my thighs together, trapping his hand with the intensity of the sensations spreading outward from my clit.

"Do you want me to stop?" His fingers stilled, pressing against my tender, hidden nub with maddening control.

"No," I whispered as my eyes fluttered open again, unable to deny the truth. I needed to come so bad, needed him to move his fingers, to slip them beneath my bottoms and touch me inside. My hips shifted, begging him to move, to kiss me, do something other than stare and gloat.

He smiled. So arrogant. So in control. "Your beautiful pussy belongs to me." He swept a circle around my engorged sex, causing me to shudder with the sweet sensation of his possession. "No matter how far you run or where you try to hide, no one will ever make you feel this way. No one but me," he said, his searing gaze pinning mine. He was claiming me, reminding me that I belonged to him and him alone. Forever.

Dickhead. Like I didn't already know.

"Come for me, Casey," he commanded and sliding his fingers up and under the stretchy fabric of my bottoms, he probed my wet slit. "Come for me. Now."

His tongue entered my mouth as his finger pressed inside my slick entrance. The combined assault thrust me over the edge in a powerful surge that left me no choice but to obey his command. He caught my ecstatic cry with his lips, pressing his mouth firm against mine, tasting the heat that consumed me. Pleasure spiraled as my body spasmed, clutching his finger as if it were his cock. My chest heaved as I trembled, while wave after wave of intense pleasure rippled from my core.

He held me close, locked in his strong arms, shielding me with his big body, his mouth trailing kisses along my jaw, while slowly the seat beneath me became solid again and the world stopped spinning.

"Feel better?" he whispered by my ear, his breath hot and uneven.

I nodded against his shoulder, unable to do more, my body weak from the orgasm still sizzling through my veins.

"Wow," Astrid said with a little cough. "You guys have *got* to be members of the mile-high club. Do you even *know* you're in a public place? Hell," she added with a grin in her voice. "At least you didn't make her cry, Lucas."

Startled, we shifted apart, his hand slipping from between my legs, both of us still breathing hard.

"What do you want, Ass-turd?" Lucas asked with an irritated sigh. He kept his back to her, and his gaze locked on me, studying my flushed face and bent bunny whiskers with arrogant satisfaction as my skin slowly cooled.

"Well, I hate to interrupt, and I seriously do hate to, my sweets..." Her eyes went wide as her gaze met mine, and she mouthed a silent '*OMG!*' as she pantomimed with her fingers what she thought she'd just walked in on. "But it's been over twenty minutes," she said, switching to counting a list on her fingers as Lucas turned to look at her. "The natives are getting restless. That Bat Guy won't leave my ass alone. And *you* turned off your phone," she accused, glaring at me. "How was I supposed to know if you were dead or alive?"

"Someone's actually interested in your bony ass?" Lucas asked with a grin. "Do I need to have a talk with him? Teach him some taste in women?"

Astrid's jaw dropped. She planted her hands on her model-thin hips. "You are such a loser."

"Is he bugging you?" I asked. My pulse had slowed to the point I could talk.

"Who? Him?" she pointed at Lucas. "He always bugs me. You know that."

Yeah, they were like brother and sister, joking around at each other's expense, but when push came to shove, they'd back each other up, if only for me.

"No," I said, smiling. "Bat Guy."

"Well…no. He's kind of….um, hot. You need to come and meet him," she gestured at me excitedly. "I think he's rich. He's staying here at the hotel in the Presidential Suite and he says he has a summer home in Sweden."

Lucas rolled his eyes. "All vital qualities in a potential mate, I'm sure." He caught my gloved fingers in his and brought them to his lips, touching my knuckles with light kisses that I felt all the way to my heart.

Pathetic how little I could resist him, but that didn't mean he owned me. And if he thought he'd gotten the upper hand by making me come at his command, well, I was the one who'd had a lovely, intense orgasm, now wasn't I? While he was left with an erection the size of Mt. Everest.

He rose to let me escape from the table and stretched, puffing out his chest like a guy supremely pleased with himself, his jeans pressing tight across his already tight package. If the obvious size of his hard-on embarrassed him, he didn't look it as he stood there, waiting for me to pass.

I patted his crotch as I slid by him to leave, brushing against his body on my way. "You should probably get that checked out. Packing concealed weapons is a felony."

He grinned. "We'll finish this later," he said, catching my eye with a hungry, meaningful look.

"Will we?" I teased with a smirk and grabbed my jacket and belt. Turning my back on him, I headed toward the bathroom with Astrid in tow, yammering on about the Bat Guy, though I barely heard what she said.

My hair was a mess, my lipstick gone if the smears all over Lucas's face were anything to go by, and my body hummed from a delicious, naughty interlude with the man I desperately loved. The nausea was history, my stomach all fluttery with excitement. I felt so hungry I could probably have eaten a whole cheesecake.

But what I truly hungered for, of course, was Lucas.

Maybe he thought he'd won by dominating me

so easily, but my taste lingered in his mouth, my scent on his skin. He'd be thinking of me for the rest of the afternoon, with that big raging hard-on. It wouldn't take much to push him over the edge. He'd see things my way about this marriage problem, and then we'd have some hot make-up sex.

I was sure of it.

Drawing Lessons

"LUCAS, YOU CAN sit here at the laptop. Projector's plugged in and ready to go, but I thought we'd start with a bit of Q and A from the audience before you do your demo." The M.C. for our next scheduled session directed as he hurried us to the presentation table set up on the stage. "Casey, you'll sit here between us."

"Thanks, Jeff." I flashed him a grateful smile as he pulled out my chair for me.

I sat down with a relieved sigh. Due to the extra

hour we'd spent at the signing, I'd barely had the chance for a quick dash to the washroom before heading to this event. The large conference room was already packed, the crowd buzzing with excitement, but the doors were still open for last minute stragglers. We had a moment or two before the show would begin.

Perched on my chair, I rolled my shoulders and neck. The long afternoon had left me sore and irritable, but the tight strings and buckles of my corset were impossible to adjust by myself and Astrid, done for the day, had gone off for a dinner date with her sexy new Bat-friend.

I caught Jeff watching me as I raised my gloved arms, stretching them over my head to relieve some tension. His gaze froze as my cleavage thrust upward, a deep blush creeping from the fringe of his ginger-colored neck beard.

Smiling, I relaxed my posture and tugged my bodice back into place. I didn't mind the heat of his stare or that he was looking, but there was only one man whose interest I really craved.

Lucas flipped open the laptop as he seated himself on my other side. He might have offered to adjust my costume and massage my stiff muscles, if he'd cared to notice my discomfort. But right now, his attention seemed thoroughly occupied with obnoxiously-helpful Hyacinth and her too-cute dimples.

He paused, mesmerized by her gracefulness as she bent down, placing a fresh pitcher of ice water—specially made for him with lemon slices and what appeared to be sprigs of fresh mint—on the table. She was trim and sleek, the complete opposite of me. Clearly, she worked out to have a body that tight. And clearly, he enjoyed it.

I drummed my fingers on the table trying to decide what to do. My mood had steadily degraded from brazenly optimistic after our sexy restaurant interlude to downright ticked.

Being friendly was part of Lucas's job as much as it was mine. He was very good at making each of the fans feel special. But there was special and then there was *special,* and the way Hyacinth had glued herself to his side, laughing at his jokes and puffing up his ego like a goddamn groupie, it seemed the line had been more than crossed. It'd been trampled out of existence. Perhaps his original plan had been to make me mildly jealous. Teach me a lesson about what I was missing.

But at some point in the last couple of hours his raging hard-on had disappeared, and I had the sneaking suspicion who'd helped him perform that magic act. I also had the sneaking suspicion I hated her for it.

"Can I get you anything else, Mr. Haskell?" Hyacinth asked with a not-very-subtle wink. The invitation was so blatant she might as well have licked her slutty lips at him.

I tried not to imagine it, but the vision of her mouth wrapped around his gorgeous, veined erection grew agonizingly large in my mind, as did the bitterness twisting my stomach.

Call it what you will: my wicked weakness, my sinful obsession, but I loved sucking Lucas's cock. It had come as a bit of a surprise to both of us as I hadn't enjoyed it with other men, but from the first time I'd tried fellatio with Lucas, I hadn't been able get enough. I didn't know if it was his taste, or his scent, or the sense of power his reaction gave me, but sucking him off was one of my favorite sexual things to do and the thought of someone else doing it with him instead of me? That nausea I'd been fighting all day surged back like a hot, bilious wave, ticking me off even more.

You'd think Lucas would pick up on my obvious irritation, but like an idiot, he smiled at Hyacinth, gracing her with the full force of his manly-man gaze. "Thanks for offering," he said, his voice all warm and charming. "But I'm fine right now. Maybe later?"

Maybe LATER???

Fuck this shit.

Leaning forward in my chair, I snagged Hyacinth's attention with a little two-fingered wave. "Hey there…Remember me? Casey Jackson." I pointed at my chest. "You know, the other person you're supposed to be fawning over? Well, here's the thing," I said, fighting to keep my words civil. "You need to leave. Now. We're about to start the demo." I pointed toward the attendants who were beginning to close the doors.

Her dimples disappeared, her perky smile fading as she backed away from the table. She glanced uncertainly at Lucas, seeking support, but his scowling glare was trained directly on me. Ha! If he thought I was being a bitch, I didn't really care. I was tired, and sore and sick to my stomach and how the hell old was she anyway? Nineteen? Twenty?

Seriously…Fuck. This. Shit.

"Oh, and another thing. Don't bother coming back, especially not *later*," I added as I poured a glass of water from the pitcher she'd brought specially for him. "Lucas is a big boy. He can take care of himself."

Raising the glass in a mock gesture of thanks, I threw her a tart smile and took a long sip.

It was difficult to hear her outraged gasp over the loud murmur buzzing through the room, but I did get the satisfaction of seeing her perky ass bolting for the exit as she hurried to leave.

"That wasn't very nice." Deep and tinged with anger, Lucas's voice caused the hairs on my neck to prickle as his hot breath caressed my ear.

"No?" I put the glass down, resisting the urge to turn to him as that intoxicating scent of his filled my head. His taste was still on my lips from earlier and despite him being a bastard, I craved him. "She's so hot for you flames are shooting out of her twat. Someone had to cool her down. You're lucky I didn't dump that pitcher over her head."

"You wouldn't be feeling jealous, would you, Casey?"

Unable to resist anymore, I turned from the crowd to glare at him. "You wouldn't be trying to make me, would you Lucas?"

"You started this by leaving." His eyes locked on mine, pinning the blame for this mess on me. "Are you ready to end it and come back?"

"Are you ready to stop being a dick and give up on this stupid idea of marriage?"

"You've belonged to me since the moment we

met. Why not make it legal?"

"Because monogamy is a two-way street," I snapped. "And you seem to have driven off the road. How long did you wait after finger-fucking me before your little friend sucked your cock?"

His brows rose at the accusation, his eyes like sparks of blue fire. "Jesus Christ, Casey. She's just a playful kid." His nostrils flared as he swept me with a look of raw hunger. "All I can smell is you. All I can think of is *you*." He shook his head, his jaw clenching tight. "You make me so fucking crazy I already rubbed one out in the john."

Oh, holy hell.

Mouth hanging open, I stared at him, incredulous, elated, and seriously turned on all at the same time. "Rubbed one out?" I asked as my brain lurched into action. "You mean you—"

"Yes," he hissed, quickly covering the little jerking motion I was making with my hand. "And don't you fucking laugh," he snapped as a grin split my face. He glanced at the crowd, spots of color dotting his cheeks.

"I'm not." I wrapped my hand over my mouth, trying not to giggle as relief swept through me that I'd been wrong about Hyacinth. "I'm just—damn. If you couldn't wait, I would have helped you out."

"On your knees in a goddamn stall? You're better than that, Casey."

"Oh, baby." My voice dipped to a husky drawl as warmth spread through me at the back-handed praise in his chastisement. "I'd be on my knees right now, if I could wedge myself under the table." It had a floor length cloth covering the front side to shield our legs from view. It could work.

His gaze fell on my glossy red lips and the intense longing that flashed in his eyes was almost my undoing.

A polite cough from Jeff snapped us back to reality.

"Ah...sorry guys," he interrupted. "If you're ready, I'll do a quick introduction...?"

I glanced at the full rows of seats, realizing just how closely together we'd been sitting, whispering our passionate debate while the crowd watched. My cheeks heated as I gave the sea of faces a little wave, evoking a rumble of chuckles from the mostly male crowd. A few women sat scattered throughout the audience but no one under eighteen had been allowed in due to the focus on anatomy and the naked human form. This wasn't a kids seminar. The demonstration was meant for comic art fans, here to learn tricks from a pro.

"Go ahead," Lucas said with a stiff nod at Jeff. He twirled the stylus in his fingers and tapped it on the tablet plugged into his laptop, the look in his eyes intense, his shoulders rigid.

He was about to do a live drawing demonstration for a crowd of about fifty-odd strangers, his every recorded move uploaded and dissected on YouTube faster than I could blink. He'd done it before to good review, but was it any wonder his jaw was clenched and his body full of cagey energy?

What the hell was I thinking? My job had always been to keep him grounded. Acting like a silly, jealous biatch was doing nothing but setting him off.

Taking a deep breath, I mentally regrouped and shoved my anxieties aside. Whatever our differences, we were still the Lucas and Casey Show and we needed to be on. In top form. Right now. Which for Lucas meant some serious distraction needed to happen to help him relax in front of the crowd.

So, while Jeff listed off our credentials to the audience, I tapped into the erotic energy dancing between us and offered Lucas something to think about besides the sea of eyes staring at him.

Placing my hand on his knee where no one could see it beneath the table, I slowly slid it up his thigh and bent toward his ear again. "You got this, babe," I murmured. "I'm sorry for being cranky, it's just…" I bit my lip as my voice hitched with the serious desires twisting me up. "I'm dying inside without you. I really need to taste your cock." My mouth went dry just thinking about the way he groaned as he found release, the fire in his eyes as he filled me with his love.

"Casey," he said, his voice a low rasp. He kept

his fingers busy on top of the table, playing with his stylus, his face a smiling mask for the crowd. "When this shit's over, I'm going to fuck you so hard you'll never leave me again." And the look in his eyes as he glanced sideways at me left no doubt that as soon as we were alone, he'd make good on his promise.

Thrilled to see his raging hard-on had returned, I cupped the outline of his stiff cock through his denim jeans and gave it a little 'yes, please' squeeze.

My body tingled with excitement, recharging my mood considerably. If he thought he could tame me by fucking me six ways to Sunday, I was all game. The plan was perfect except for one tiny detail. Hot sex didn't change the fact I couldn't marry him.

"So, if anyone has any questions before we move on to the demonstration, I'll open the floor to Lucas and Casey," Jeff said, passing over the microphone to us.

A hand shot up in the front row where a college-age fanboy sat with his friends.

Lucas nodded for him to go ahead.

"When did you know you wanted to draw comics for a living?"

"Probably forever," he answered, his rich, velvety voice magnified a hundred times as it boomed from the speakers. "I was the kid always drawing in class. The teachers hated it, but it's how I practiced." He grinned. "I'm not saying math isn't important, but when the ideas come, you have to work them through."

Fanboy nodded as if he knew exactly what Lucas was talking about. "That's cool," he said, grinning, and sat back down in his seat.

Another hand shot up. The girl it was attached to stood and smiled at me. "Casey, as woman working in a man's world…what are the most annoying things you see in comic books?"

"Aside from poorly drawn hands and feet?" Tapping my finger against my lips, I looked thoughtfully around the room. "I'd have to say…gratuitously large breasts."

A snicker rippled through the crowd as everyone

stared at mine. Grinning, I looked at Lucas as the laughter quieted down. "What do you think?" I asked him. "Can breasts be too large?"

His brow lifted, his gaze narrowing as it slid from my eyes to my rack. "They can be tricky to handle," he agreed, and the crowd burst into laughter again.

This banter was part of the show, our way of connecting the crowd, but I stared at him dumbfounded as he suddenly held out the drawing pen.

"Why don't you show them what you mean?" he asked, a mischievous smile spreading across his face.

"What?" I gaped at him, my face heating. "You want *me* to draw?"

He shrugged. "Stick figures are fine."

I glared at the stylus dangling from his fingers as if it were a poisonous snake. Lucas drew. I distracted. That's the way it had always been. That's the way it should be now. Was this a joke? Was he trying to humiliate me? Or did he want the world to see that I was more than a pretty face?

"Come on," he coaxed, challenge clear in his smoldering eyes. "Show us what you've got."

"You are a *very* stupid man," I hissed low enough only he could hear. *Show us what you've got.* Idiot. I'd show them all what I was made of, most especially him.

The crowd clapped as I grabbed the stylus from him and stood.

A smug smile tipping his lips, Lucas started to move in order to switch seats with me, but I stopped him with a push from my stiletto-heeled boot to his chest.

"Oh no," I said as his surprised gaze travelled the length of my raised leg and froze on the unobstructed view I'd given him of my velveteen-covered crotch. "You can stay right where you are."

Keeping my gaze fixed on him, I stepped back, slowly undid my gun belt and slipped out of my long coat. It slid to the floor in a sinuous pool of leather, baring my tightly corseted figure to the admiring gaze of the crowd. Wolf whistles thrilled my ears, making my heart race with pleasure as everyone's eyes, including Lucas's, studied my voluptuous curves.

His smoldering gaze licked my naked flesh, glowing white in the bright glare of the spotlights trained on the stage. I shivered from the intense heat as every part of my body reveled in the unabashed hunger burning from him. Exposed, unrepressed the sizzling need sparking between us burned my skin as I squeezed by the table and settled onto his lap.

Straddling his left leg, I leaned back against him. He sucked in a sharp breath as my tail bunched between us, pressing against his erection. One of his hands jerked over my thigh to grasp my hip. The other slid across my waist, his fingers fanning outward to span the width of my stomach and hold me in place.

"What the hell are you doing?" he whispered by my ear.

"Showing you what I've got," I said, with an impish grin. "You asked me to, didn't you?"

A low growl rumbled through his chest. His

fingers tightened on my hip. "You are *not* taking off anymore clothes," he added in a harsh whisper by my ear. "Not for anyone but me." His hand slipped from my hip and slid down my center, his long fingers plunging into the grooves on either side of my mound. "*This* is mine. You are *mine*. Behave yourself, Casey," he warned, and he gave my pussy a little scissor pinch.

I almost shot off his lap with the intense pleasure that zinged to my core, but he held me in place, his hand tight on my stomach. Straddled the way I was over his thigh, I couldn't close my legs. I was completely at his mercy and I loved every daring minute of it. So did he, judging by the hardness of his erection pressed against my ass. Sitting like this, I'd given him control over my body and I had no doubt that he'd use it if I strayed too far.

He kept his hand in place on my sex, ready to "punish" me again as I turned back to the crowd. Trembling with the desire to seriously misbehave, I licked my suddenly dry lips.

"So…" I said into the microphone. The shadow

of my hand grew large in the square of projected light on the screen as I raised the stylus above the tablet. "Breasts."

I bit my lip to stifle a nervous giggle and started to draw, my hand shaking slightly as I gained a new appreciation for the fine art of distraction. "Well, to begin with, breasts aren't circles," I said. I quickly drew a stick figure example of a torso with hard melon-ball breasts and put a large "x" through it. "The bottom is heavier, the top a gentle curve, but they can be any shape. Full, thin, you name it." I started on another, more realistic version of a torso, like something out of a *Grey's Anatomy* textbook, demonstrating how a properly proportioned chest looked and the fact that I might not have Lucas's talent, but I could draw. "The important thing to remember is they have weight and change shape when you move. Just like an erection."

Laughter rippled from the crowd. Growling low, Lucas pressed his fingers along the sides of my mound, warning me he was still in control and what would happen if I didn't behave.

Wickedness gripped me as I started on another pose of a woman bending forward, her full, tight-nippled breasts suspiciously close to mine. The scissor pinch came hard and fast, sucking the breath from my lungs with a sharp gasp. I jerked, pressing down on his thigh, my folds spasming as moisture seeped between them.

Holy hell. He was going to get a soaked leg if he kept that up.

Keeping my breathing as steady as possible, I grappled for composure as I studied the enraptured crowd. "But seriously, guys. Breasts are *heavy*. Drawing a woman with a tiny chest and boobs the size of giant melons? It doesn't work." I tapped the stylus on my first drawing as a chuckle rippled through the crowd. "You're going to break her back if you don't give her some kind of support. And believe me, corsets are not comfortable. So, unless anti-gravity breasts are *supposed* to be her super-power, don't go there."

Smiling, I put the stylus down, done with my lesson and about ready to explode if Lucas didn't stop the gentle soothing rubs his fingers were doing on the sides of my pussy.

"There you go, guys," Jeff said into the mic. "Breasts are heavy, so don't forget to draw them that way." He smiled at the chuckles rippling through the audience. "Let's give Casey a round of applause for her, ah, enlightening demonstration." His gaze flicked downward at Lucas's hand between my legs and back at me, his brow lifting with an appreciative smile.

Perhaps I should have been embarrassed that he'd witnessed our naughty game, but as the room echoed with clapping and whistles, all I could think about was Lucas, the feel of his strong thigh pressed between mine and how much this man of mine made me burn.

All the hurt and resentment had melted away, leaving just me and him and our raging need to be together.

His arms wrapped tight around me, pulling me against him. "You did great, Casey. I'm proud of you," he murmured by my ear, his voice a hot whisper. "Do you like my distraction?"

A slow, languorous slide of his fingers had me gripping the table. "You do awesome distraction," I agreed with a gasp.

"Good." He kissed me on my temple, a tiny peck that nearly stopped my heart. "As soon as we're alone, I'll give you my *full* attention."

Stars bloomed in front of my eyes as he slid his fingers along my slit. I shuddered, barely able to contain my moan, wanting nothing more than for the crowd to disappear so I could unzip his fly and sink down onto his hard, waiting cock.

"We're running a bit tight on time," Jeff said, looking at his phone. "But before Lucas gives us his demonstration, there's something that everyone here wants to know. We've all heard the rumors..." he smiled at the audience and then looked at me. "Casey, it is true that you're leaving *Steam Bunny*?"

My smile froze.

Lucas's hand slipped from between my legs and clutched the table instead. I gave Jeff my best death glare as all the happy feelings bubbling inside abruptly died. If I could have force-choked him like Darth Vader having a hissy-fit, I would have. My employment status was *not* on our list of prepared answers and he knew it. But he held the microphone out to me, brows raised, waiting while I floundered.

"I…well, I…" I looked over my shoulder at Lucas, a tumult of emotions churning inside. He stared back at me, silent and pensive, his expression tight with the tension pounding between us.

Would I leave? Should I leave? Could I stay? I didn't want this to end, but we hadn't reached an agreement yet.

He wanted all or nothing.

I wanted the fire and passion, the choice to be with him every day. *Not* because a piece of paper and a gold band said we had to. Forced together until either we died, or our love became jaded? Where was the romance in that?

The silence stretched as we stared into each other's eyes and I had the horrible feeling mine were glistening with the beginnings of tears. The indecision twisted, squeezing the breath from my lungs. Blinking, I shook my head, trying to clear it, my fingers digging into his thighs.

It was so unfair dumping this moment on me. My words to say. My path to take. Why wouldn't Lucas step in and help me? Say something. Anything to take the heat off my back. But he continued watch me in silence, hope and anticipation searing his gaze, his lips a hard line as he waited for me to choose.

"Well," said Jeff into the awkward gap. "Looks like they're still negotiating terms."

I swallowed hard, pulse thundering as bitter disappointment settled over Lucas, turning his handsome face into a wooden mask.

Fuck. I couldn't leave things like this. Not like *this*.

Sucking in a deep breath I grabbed the mic as something inside me snapped. "No." My choked whisper echoed around the room, buzzing in my ears. Ignoring my thundering heart, and the fist of sickness hitting my stomach, I smiled at the crowd. "I'm not leaving," I said more strongly. "Not yet," I qualified.

"Fantastic!" Jeff exclaimed. Smiling at the crowd, he started everyone clapping.

Nausea washed over me with the ramifications of what I'd just done. There'd be hell to pay for that white lie, but I'd saved face for us in front of the crowd and this, right now, was about business. Right? *Right?*

It certainly seemed to be, with the overwhelming reaction from the audience. Shouts and cheers, and smiles of approval? Did our relationship really matter that much? It did if Race Lindstrom was in that crowd, watching the uproar my announcement had made. This could make or break that *Steam Bunny* TV deal, taking our future with it.

Lucas's arms locked about me, holding me tight against him again, tension easing from him like a wave. But what had felt warm and passionate moments before, now seemed to choke the air from my lungs.

"You okay?" he whispered beside my ear.

"Nope," I admitted, avoiding his gaze. I couldn't

seem to steady my pulse, no matter how many deep yoga breaths I took.

"We'll make it okay," he said and gave my shoulder a little kiss. "You'll see."

I didn't get how that would ever be possible, given that I'd just lied to him in front of a room full of fans. Pushing at him, I tried to stand, but his hand caught my jaw, forcing me to look at him.

"I love you, Casey," he said, his eyes piercing my soul with the intensity of his conviction. "Do you think I don't understand what you just did?"

The elation in his voice grated my nerves like fingernails on a chalkboard. Clearly, he didn't understand. He thought he'd won. He believed the lie. The sickness inside built as my stomach tightened, making me tremble. If I didn't get away from him soon, I'd puke.

"Are you ready for some drawing magic?" Jeff called out to the audience, charging them up with energy I didn't feel. With a little bow, he gave Lucas the mic. "Floor's yours, Haskell."

"Why don't you go to your room and rest?"

Lucas whispered by my ear, his voice full of concern as he helped me stand. "I'll come by as soon as I'm done."

"Lucas," I said, my voice rising as anger mixed with the guilt, sickening me. Last thing I needed was him being all sweet and treating me like a baby. "Why don't you just kiss my ass?"

The spotlights burned hot, the watching eyes seared my skin, as my request echoed around the room, magnified a hundred times.

Oh shit.

I could have walked off that stage and away from it all, but with a little two-fingered Steam Bunny salute for the crowd, I sauntered over to a nearby stool that had been set up for me to lean on so I could model for Lucas. Perching against it in my stiletto boots, I bent and struck a pose for him to draw, showing him my backside and the full glory of my half-naked ass.

The touch of lips on the curve of my butt-cheek, high up by my bunny tail, brought an explosion of whistles from the crowd and a shocked gasp from me.

I spun round.

Lucas knelt behind me, looking up at me with a broad smile on his face, microphone in hand. "Careful what you wish for," he said with a wink.

Six Ways to Sunday

HALF AN HOUR passed. Or maybe an hour and a half. I didn't know and didn't care. Time had no meaning as I sat on that stool, basking in the hot lights, my heart a throbbing ache while Lucas worked his magic.

He was in his element. Relaxed and self-assured, burning with an energy that defied anyone to not look at him, to not admire the absolute control he had over that stylus as he sketched. Blue eyes clear and bright, his easy smile full of pleasure, he oozed charisma as he joked and laughed, explaining his drawing process to the crowd. Each confident stroke of the pen left no doubt that in his mind, my curvaceous body was a beautiful thing to describe in glowing colors.

But I was not the beautiful one here.

My lungs shuddered as I remembered to breathe, the ache expanding in my chest.

He'd ditched his leather jacket. His arm muscles rippled as his strong hands flexed and shifted, his tanned skin golden beneath the bright lights. I loved touching those arms, exploring the contrast between their softness and hardness, the tickle of his short hairs against my fingers. Could I live without ever touching him again? Could I live without *him*?

Thanks to that little white lie I'd told, everyone and their cousin now believed that I was staying with *Steam Bunny*. The texts had flown far and wide. The ***#awesomeSBnews*** tweets had, more or less, gone viral. At this point, marrying Lucas was almost easier than unleashing the PR nightmare of going back on my word. Tying the knot was certainly the option that would make him the happiest. But an engaged woman should feel elated inside, shouldn't she? Whereas I felt a mixture of confused feelings, not the least of which was panic.

Lucas stood as the session wrapped up, accepting the thunderous round of applause from the crowd with a grateful bow. He looked at me and started clapping in turn, his smile radiant as I slid from my perch and dutifully blew a kiss to the fans. My stiff legs protested the sudden surge of blood flowing into them again and I clutched the stool, my smile wavering as a thousand prickles attacked my feet.

"Shit," I hissed through clenched teeth.

Lucas caught me about my waist. "Let me guess," he murmured by my ear, "Numb feet?"

I nodded, pain slicing through me so sharp I could cry. I clung to him. Normally I'd work the crowd for the next several minutes, talking with anyone who wanted to linger and ask one-on-one questions, but I couldn't do it like this. I'd been so mesmerized by Lucas, I hadn't moved a muscle. Maybe I hadn't even blinked.

"Just give me a moment," I snapped. "I'll be—"

"Come on," he interrupted, shaking his shaggy head. "Let's get you out of here." Bending low, he swept me up into his arms and off my feet, cradling me against his chest as if I were a child.

"What the—? Put me *down*." I protested with a squeak. But he wasn't letting go, and did I *really* want him to? His strength and scent were manly-awesome.

"Let's hear it for *Steam Bunny*," Jeff called out as Lucas carried me off the stage like freakin' Superman rescuing Lois Lane. The crowd started to stand, giving us an ovation as we passed down the center aisle, heading for the exit. "T-shirts and caps are available for purchase in Hall D by the—"

The door shut behind us, blocking off the rest of Jeff's spiel and replacing the thunderous applause and whistles with the quiet bustle of a hallway. Nodding to the curious attendants standing nearby, Lucas didn't even pause as he quickly ducked through an adjacent set of doors labelled 'staff only'.

A relieved smile crossed his face when a

backward glance showed the doors remained still. "Looks like we're clear."

"Yeah. Um, I can probably walk now," I said, trying not to swoon at the way his biceps bulged as he carried me down the passageway.

"Probably," he agreed. Coming to a crossway, he hesitated briefly then took the left turn. "Or I could toss you over my shoulder and spank your bunny-ass," he said with a gleam in his eye as he glanced down at me. "But then I might have to kiss it again." He made a little puckering sound with his lips.

Oh hell. "I'm sorry about that," I said. "I'm just a little—"

"High-strung?" he finished for me. "Hush, baby," he murmured into my hair. "It'll be okay. You just need some fresh air and a good hard fuck."

My mouth dropped open. "What?" I said, not certain if he was joking or if I'd even heard him right.

"Three weeks," he said. "Three fucking long weeks without you, Casey. I'm so hard right now I could tear sheet metal." He chuckled as if it were a bad joke, which it might have been except I could feel the truth of it pressing against my hip.

"I tried to be patient," he continued, "to give you some space and let you see reason, but you didn't want nice and now it's too fucking late. You're mine." Stopping in front of a set of frosted glass doors, he glanced down at me, his eyes blazing with the passionate heat radiating from his body and into mine. "Fuck waiting. I'm going to do what I should have done three weeks ago. I'm going to fuck you senseless, Casey. Right fucking now."

Hitting the latch with his knee, he shoved the door open. Cool air brushed my cheeks as he carried me through.

"That's a lot of fucks," I managed once my tongue became unglued from the roof of my mouth.

"You'd better fucking believe it." He snickered as he settled me onto a lounge chair.

I glanced around in a bit of a daze. I'd assumed we'd been heading for the elevators and back to our rooms. Instead, we were in a little rattan paradise.

The patio-style balcony was intimate in its styling. Guests could come here for a quiet cup of coffee and soak up sunshine in the fresh air. Potted palms and frosted glass walls served as dividers between the wrought iron tables, giving each setting the illusion of seclusion. Fuchsia pillows accented brown, woven chairs. A few umbrellas had been opened, offering shade to boxes of pink and white petunias decorating the concrete balustrade. We were the only people currently there, but unless the doors locked, we were far from private.

I leaned back on the lounger as an excited shiver gripped me, spreading my arms wide to catch the fragrant late afternoon breeze. "Lucas...it's *beautiful*."

A grin split his face. "I thought you'd love this little place. Bit of sunshine, some cozy pillows, and that element of risk, which drives you so wild. Anyone can walk in at any moment and catch me fucking your sweet pussy." Capturing my gloved fingers, he brought them to his lips for a hungry nibbling kiss.

"You planned this?" Heart racing, I stared at him, my mind a jumbled mess of conflicting messages. He was going to fuck me. Here? Now? But what about that little lie?

"Hell, yeah." Dropping my hand, he stepped back and quickly kicked off his shoes. "I've been thinking about it all day. That drawing lesson was serious torture." Unbuttoning his fly, he watched me as I watched him, a ravenous gleam in his eyes. "Come on, hop to it, bunny girl. Stilettos stay on. Bunny bottoms off. Now."

"But…but, Lucas," I stammered.

"No buts. Not unless were talking about yours." He grinned, a devilish flash of white teeth.

"But *Lucas*," I said more forcefully, my heart quaking as I braced for his anger. Shit. I had to tell him I wasn't really staying. Not if he still wanted marriage.

He studied me and my lack of undressing, suspicion narrowing his eyes. "Is this one of those things where you need to talk and talk and talk before we can have sex?"

Folding my arms across my chest, I gave him my sulkiest glare. "Maybe."

"Hell." Squeezing his eyes shut tight, his lips moved as he silently counted to ten. "Okay, Casey." With an impatient sigh, he sat down on the end of the lounger beside me. "What is it?"

"I lied about not leaving."

"That's all?"

"That isn't enough?"

He burst out laughing. "You weren't lying, Casey." Raising his butt off the lounger, he pushed his jeans down over his hips and began slipping them off his legs.

"I wasn't? How the hell can you—whoa..." My thoughts trailed off as his cock sprang free from his boxers. It pointed at me like an accusing finger, except much longer and thicker and holy hell, I hadn't seen it in days. I couldn't move my eyes from the gorgeous erect sight.

"Whoa," I whispered again, barely able to contain my excitement at being so close to the object of my sinful desire. "You look so good I could swallow you whole. I think I should try, just to be sure." I licked my lips, reaching for him.

"Shit." He caught my groping hands and held them away from his crotch. "Slow down, you greedy girl." His jaw clenched as tension rippled through him from the effort of resisting what we both knew would be a fantastic explosion of pleasure. "Not until you admit you weren't lying."

Seriously? I swallowed hard. "But I was lying."

He shook his head. "No, you weren't. You were telling the truth for the first time in three weeks. Why do you think you panicked so much?"

"I didn't want us to look bad. I didn't want them to know—" His lips covered mine, kissing my protest into submission. Rattan creaked as I clung to him, my hands shaking with the force of the conflicted desires gripping me. He was wrong, I didn't mean to stay unless he gave up on us getting married, but I was powerless to resist the sweep of his tongue in my mouth and the raging need coursing between us.

Thrusting his thigh between mine, he spread my

legs, nudging them off the lounger. My feet slid to either side of the chair, trapping my knees wide open for him. Tearing his mouth from mine, he glanced between our bodies at the inviting spread of my crotch.

"This is mine," he whispered in a voice so charged with emotion a sob caught my throat. He gently stroked the soft fabric covering my sex. Once. Twice. Then his hands grabbed my ass, his fingers digging in as he pulled me forward. His cock slid along my cleft, rubbing against my tender nub. Hard.

"Ahhh," I moaned, arching against the seat. My core clenched tight, the first glimmers of a powerful orgasm awakening.

"I want to marry you, Casey." He cupped my chin, forcing me to look deep into his eyes and see the truth of his conviction. "I want to wake up every morning holding the most beautiful woman in the world."

Oh God. His fingers gripped my chin so tight I couldn't look away.

"I want to make love to you every day of our lives." He ground his cock against me again, a grimace contorting his face, his eyes clouding with a mixture of pleasure and pain that I knew were reflected in mine. As a shudder ripped through me, I bit my lip, struggling to think clearly in the haze of erotic agony he'd created.

"I want to grow old with you baby," he whispered, his voice hot and hoarse. "Don't you want those things too?"

I nodded, licking my lips, unable to speak the truth in my heart, barely able to breathe.

He let go of my chin, his eyes slits of blue fire. His fingers gripped my bottoms and began tugging them down. "Take these off before I rip them."

Heart racing, I sat up and quickly did as he instructed. The fabric snagged on my thigh-high boots as my shaking hands fumbled.

Smiling at how much he'd rattled me, he helped pull them down over my stilettos, exposing my ass to the cool air and my waxed sex to his hot stare. Any vestiges of nausea vanished at the heat of that stare, leaving intense excitement. I wanted him to fuck me. I wanted him to *see.* Bending forward onto my knees, I gripped the lounger, my ass lifting high into the air.

"Gorgeous..." he murmured as if spellbound at the sight presented before him. "Perfection."

I glanced between my legs, shivering with desire at the mixture of adoration and lust stamped on his face as he examined me. My mound glistened with my need for him, the folds within hot and pink as he spread them. His tongue flicked out, tasting me with a long lick from my clit to the crease of my ass.

"*Shit.*" I bucked against him, my body jerking with spikes of pleasure as his mouth laid claim to my pussy. His tongue swirled over my sensitive skin, flicking and massaging, again, and again, his breath hot and wet. Then he speared me where I most wanted to be speared; the pulsing center of my core.

I gripped the chair, arching, unable to stop the squeezing contractions or the huffing whimpers of pleasure coming from my throat.

"No fair," I gasped as the pressure eased enough I could breathe. "You can eat me, but I can't suck you?"

He licked my taste from his lips, a wicked smile lighting his eyes. "Not until you admit you are mine."

Rimmed by the golden late afternoon light, he was like a God, his strength all-consuming as he quickly readied his cock at my entrance. In one swift thrust he embedded himself, hips deep inside me.

"Lucas," I cried out, my back arcing high at the sudden intrusion.

The sharp pain and flood of pleasure, which blossomed a second later, were almost more than I could handle. Tears stung my eyes from the joy and relief of having him within me again. I had wanted this for weeks now, been begging him for it all day. My blood pumped hot, my breath tattered as my tight channel pulsed around his swollen cock.

"Goddamn it. You feel so good," he rasped, his hands tight on my hips. "So much better than my dreams."

"Yes," I whispered in total agreement. "Oh, God, *yes*." 'Thor' was nothing compared to this.

I moaned and began to angle my hips, wanting him to thrust again, but he clamped me against him, holding us both tight together instead.

"Not until you admit that you weren't lying."

What the hell? "I can't," I moaned.

Pulling out slightly, he smacked my bare ass cheeks with his hand. Not hard enough to hurt, but sharp enough to cause a zing of pleasure rippling outward from my core.

Shocked, I glanced over my shoulder at him and caught the flare of heat in his eyes as my insides clutched his cock.

"Holy hell," I said in astonishment. "Do that again."

His lips twisted into a smile. "Tell me you weren't lying, and I will."

"Damn you," I whispered. "I can't."

His jaw hardened. "Do you really want this to be the last time we ever have sex, Casey?"

"No."

"Good." He smacked my bottom again and this time the pleasure ripples lasted longer. I wanted them to keep going forever.

Unable to take it anymore, I wiggled my ass against him. "Please, Lucas." I moaned, feeling him swell inside me. "Just fuck me."

"You want me to make you come? Is that all this is to you? A fucking ride?"

I nodded and then shook my head vigorously, confused about which way to answer. "No," I said, panting. Trapped by the corset, my swollen breasts pressed against the tight fabric of my bodice, making my erect nipples ache. "It's always been more than just sex for us. You know that."

He smacked my bottom again, this time groaning as my core milked his cock in an undulating spasm of sharp ripples. I was going to orgasm soon, just from the pleasure of having him inside me.

"Sweet heaven, you're wet," he groaned.

"You make me that way."

"See? You're lying about leaving. Admit it."

Slipping a hand to my mound, he touched where we were joined and smeared my slick cream around the base of his cock. His thumb slid upward, brushing my clit. I cried out, arching backward against him, as he stroked my sensitive nub. Stars flashed behind my closed lids as he held himself rigid inside me, despite my quaking body.

"Say it quickly," he commanded. "If someone shows up, this is all over."

"No." I cried out, panic gripping my frazzled brain that he might leave without finishing what we'd started.

"Is that your answer?"

"No!" I cried out again fighting not to cry from the intensity of it all: the lust to have him, the need to be free, his desperate attempt at persuasion. "Please, Lucas," I begged, wanting him to end the ache in the most primal way possible.

"Choice is yours, Casey," he said, his voice a rough growl. His thighs shook with the strain of keeping me embedded and both of us under control. "Say you'll come with me forever, or this will be the last time."

He thrust deep, hard and urgent, giving me no choice but to take the pleasure and burn with it.

"Yes," I screamed as the orgasm hit me, a tight, almost painful release that had my sex clutching his cock in a grasping, undulating rhythm. A second peak built close on the first, less sharp but more intense as he pumped within my swollen, sensitive channel.

Hard and fast, his fingers biting into my hips, his breathing ragged. Rattan creaked in protest. My arms and knees strained to hold me. The wonderful, beautiful glory of it filled me, clawing at my insides, too soon. I wanted to make it last but...Oh, God. Oh, *God.*

"Lucas." I cried his name to the sky, my voice breaking on a sob. I didn't care who heard me. I never wanted this to end.

"Shit, shit, shit," he hissed. "You're too sexy and tight." His rhythm became short and jerky, mirroring his breathing.

I flexed my hips, knowing he was close, and

clutched him from the inside.

"Yes, baby. *Yes.*" His hand slid over my wet pussy lips, his fingers finding my clit. Rubbing hard, he pressed down.

I gasped.

"Casey," he groaned as we came hard together, our bodies jerking until my arms threatened to snap. "Oh God, *Casey.*"

There wasn't enough breath left in my lungs to shout the joy of sharing that precious moment with him. But I managed a delighted whimper as his hands spasmed on my ass while he poured himself into me.

His thrusts slowed. Capturing me tight in his arms, his ragged breaths filled my ears, as we sank, spent and weak, onto the lounger.

"Don't you ever leave me again," he ordered.

"I won't," I promised.

Rolling to face him, I stroked lines of sweat from his handsome, exhausted face, not caring if it stained my gloves. I was going to need a new pair anyway, with the mess the rattan had made of the satin. I smiled. Wrapping my arms around him, I cradled his head against my breasts, the corset straining to contain them as I slowly caught my breath.

"I won't leave," I said again, feeling the truth of my conviction bloom in my soul. How the hell could I ever be without a man like Lucas? "It's just...marriage scares the everlasting shit out of me."

His eyes cracked open. A smile touched his lips. "I'm not like your father, you know. Not every guy is a deadbeat asshole."

"I know that."

"Then why are you treating me like one?"

"I'm—what? I'm not. No really, I'm not," I insisted at his cocked brow. He wasn't an asshole like my father. But I didn't want marriage to turn him into one, either.

With a heavy sigh, he left the satin embrace of my arms and sat up. Grabbing a couple of napkins from the nearby table, he reached between my legs and gently wiped at the sticky mess he'd left there. I jerked as his fingers brushed my tender skin.

"Sorry," he said, sounding not sorry at all. "I couldn't hold back. It's been a while."

I giggled. The full load required lots of wiping, not that I minded his gentlemanly ministrations in the slightest. We hadn't used a condom since the first week we'd been together and proven we were clean and committed. I took it as a good sign he hadn't used one now.

"Can I clean you too?" I asked, licking my lips suggestively.

Tossing the used napkins into a nearby trash bin, he looked me deep in the eyes. "Will you marry me, Casey?"

Ouch. Nothing like cutting right to the point. "I want to, Lucas," I admitted, finding my voice without hesitation for once. "But I need more time to think about it. It's a big step for me, you know?"

"Yeah, I know." His expression hardened. Shaking his head, he busied himself with pulling his boxers on again. "If three weeks isn't long enough, how much time do you need?"

"I honestly don't know," I answered with all the honesty I could.

"Yeah? Well that's a problem, 'cause neither do I."

He stood. Finding his pants, he quickly pulled them on.

I flinched as he angrily zipped up his fly. "Why are you so mad?" Hadn't I just said I was staying? That'd I'd consider the idea of marriage?

"I'm tired of all your bullshit, Casey," he snapped. "This, right here," he gestured between us with a flourish, "This is *love*." Stepping toward me, he grabbed me by the arms, pulling me to my feet. "I *love* you, Casey." Staring into my eyes, he gave me a little shake. "Why doesn't that matter to you?"

"It does matter," I insisted. "It's everything to me. *You're* everything to me, Lucas."

"Then stop letting your stupid insecurities get in the way." He fished in his jeans pocket and pulled out the ring he'd shown me three weeks ago.

"Take this. I can make you happy, you know that. We'll fly down to Vegas on Monday and—"

"Vegas?" I took the ring and held it up. He'd kept it in his *pocket?* The diamond sparkled in the light, a thousand flashes of hopes and dreams, making me blink. I folded my hand over it and held it to my breast as the ache in my heart swelled. "I need more time," I whispered, nausea fluttering in my stomach.

"Right. Of course." He let go of me and backed away with a sharp nod, his expression filling with pain. "You know what? Keep the ring. Sell it if you want to. I don't give a fuck anymore."

Turning toward the door, he ran a hand through his hair, the silky strands slipping through his fingers in a gesture of resignation as he slipped his shoes on.

He was leaving. *He was leaving.*

"Please don't," I begged, my whole body shaking. I couldn't connect with the reality of what was happening. How did we go from erotic bliss to this? "Lucas," I called out as he reached the door. "I'm sorry." Tears ran down my cheeks, unhindered and unwanted, but very much real.

"I'm not," he said, his face set in a stony mask. "I guess that's the difference between us."

He opened the door and walked through it, shutting it behind him.

"Oh God," I whispered as an ominous quiet settled over the balcony. Street noises filled the air. The breeze gently ruffled an umbrella awning. But without Lucas filling the space with his familiar presence, the little idyll seemed empty.

He'd be back in a moment, wouldn't he? Bringing me my jacket? He wouldn't just fuck me and leave me out here alone, no matter how hard we'd argued.

Putting my bunny bottoms back on, I sat on the lounger, watching while the shadows crept out from beneath the tables and chairs as the sun slowly sank below the towering spires of Chicago.

At one point the door opened, making me jerk with a rush of excitement, but it was just a hotel server, coming by to fasten the umbrellas for the night.

"Can I get you anything?" she asked, her smile

politely curious.

"No, thank you. I'd like to just sit here."

"Sure. The patio closes at ten p.m."

I nodded and she left, leaving me alone with my aching heart.

As the last flares of sunlight vanished and patio lanterns flickered on like ghostly sentinels, I shivered. I was cold and hungry and pretty sure I'd lost my chance at a happy life.

The despair cut deeper than tears could ever fix.

Lucas was gone and he wasn't coming back.

That Bitch Called Karma

"IT SAYS…IT says…*Eat Me*," Astrid said, looking at the card room service had delivered along with a continental breakfast, carafe of orange juice, and a bouquet of twelve very pretty edible chocolate roses.

"And it doesn't say who it's from?" I took a long sip of the juice she had passed me and immediately wished I hadn't. My stomach apparently considered O.J. a demon that must be exorcised. Placing the glass on the bedside table, I lay down on my side again as she flipped the card over and shook her head.

"Nope. But I bet it was Lucas." A little mischievous smile pulled at her lips. "Eat me…that sounds kinda suggestive. Maybe it's an invitation?"

"Maybe," I agreed, but I didn't share her enthusiasm.

I hadn't seen Lucas since he'd stormed off the patio. My texts had gone unanswered, my calls straight to his voicemail. Pressing my ear to the door of his room last night, the sound of voices and music had made my stomach clench. He was there, but was he alone? Hoping it was just the TV, I'd knocked, then knocked again more loudly. The door had remained shut. I hadn't tried a third time.

I'd lain in bed, staring at the ceiling after that, certain I'd never sleep with the misery eating my soul. Yet hopeful that if I left the door unlocked on my side of our adjoining suite, maybe he'd get over his anger and join me.

But I'd woken just the same, lonely, heartsick and alone, when Astrid had come back this morning. She'd spent a truly erotic night—if the fuck-bruise finger pattern ringing her arms and the hickeys on her neck were any clue—with the ass-grabber himself, Bat Guy.

"Maybe it's from your Caped Crusader?" I asked with a wink, trying for her sake to be chipper.

A blush tinted Astrid's cheeks as she put the card on the silver service tray, picked a petal from a chocolate rose and popped it in her mouth. Her eyes shone bright as she looked at me, the early morning sunlight filtering through the drapery of our hotel room setting off the blond highlights in her hair like a halo. She was no angel when it came to her sexuality, but she wasn't promiscuous either, and despite my own troubles, I felt genuinely happy she'd had some fun last night. Her last relationship had ended nine months ago when the guy in question turned out to be Mr. Unfaithful instead of Mr. Wonderful.

"Oh my God, Casey!" she squealed. "What if it is?" She did a little happy dance around the breakfast bar and over to my bed.

"Then I'd say he's more than just a pair of cute

bat ears." I grinned at her excitement. Astrid had introduced us at the signing and the guy had been *built*, tall too. No need to wear any foam padding to fill out the muscles for that costume. Coupled with a lantern jaw and piercing blue eyes, he really could have been Bat Guy. "You never found out his real name?"

"No." She turned crimson, still embarrassed by having spent the night with a complete stranger hours after first meeting him. She sat down on the edge of my bed where I lay curled up in my robe. Not that it was any surprise considering my constantly nauseous state these days, but that orange juice wasn't settling well at all.

"I never asked," she admitted. "It was so much sexier to keep pretending he was Bat Guy. He never took his mask off the whole night." A giggle escaped her at some memory of the evening's events she'd kept private. "You were soooo right, Casey. Role playing is a *huge* turn-on."

"Only with the right guy."

I grinned, remembering the first time Lucas had

helped me get dressed as Steam Bunny and how fast he'd undressed me again. His reaction to the bits of leather and lace clinging to my body had been such a turn-on for us both. We hadn't gotten any work done that afternoon, but we'd made a lot of good memories. Of course, it seemed that memories were all we'd have now, because I was pretty sure I'd really fucked things up.

"Well," I said, my smile slipping as my gaze strayed back to the incriminating evidence I held in my hand that Karma was indeed a bitch. "What the hell am I supposed to do now?"

The little plus sign on the pregnancy test stared back at me, just as vivid as when I'd raced to the bathroom this morning, hand clamped over my mouth as I gagged, and taken the test. And then, because it was a two-pack, I'd done a second one a bit later, just to make certain that Karma wasn't joking. Naturally, she wasn't.

"Oh, Casey!" Astrid's arm wrapped around my shoulders in a comforting hug. "I'm so sorry. Here I am giggling like a schoolgirl while you...you're..."

"I'm pregnant." I finished for her.

"You're pregnant," she whispered, her eyes glistening as she stared at the test in my hand.

We'd been here before, ten years earlier, only the test had been in her shaking hand then, not mine. The pain and anxiety of that time still haunted her, a shadow dimming the brightness of her blue eyes. I roused myself and gave her a tight hug too.

"You okay?" I whispered.

She nodded, pulling away to wipe her eyes and paste on a smile. "Sure," she chirped. "Why wouldn't I be? My best friend's going to have a sweet little *bay-bee*." And maybe a tiny bit of sparkle did light her eyes. "It's good news. Right?"

"Yeah," I said, unsure that it was.

I'd been mulling it over for days, wondering how this moment would be if I took a test and it was positive. Kids were something I'd always assumed I'd have someday. I'd just never expected someday to be now. We'd been careful with birth control, but apparently even pills weren't a hundred percent. Would I have been disappointed if it had turned out negative? Maybe. Lucas was crazy about kids. I hoped.

"But it'd be a hell of a lot better if the daddy didn't hate me."

"Don't be stupid," Astrid said, her smile faltering. "He doesn't hate you. Once he cools down, you'll see. You just need to sit together and talk."

"Easier said than done when he won't speak to me, let alone listen."

She shook her head. "Did you try again this morning?"

"No."

I twirled the engagement ring on my finger, spinning the diamond setting round and round. I'd been trying it on intermittently to see how it looked. Who knew the weight on my finger would make me feel special rather than choked? Slipping it off again, I put it on my bedside table, sadness over all I'd lost prickling my eyes with tears.

"I don't think it really matters anymore," I whispered.

"*Casey*," Astrid snapped. "Of course it matters. Especially right now. So you argued? So what? It's not the first time. Do you love him?"

"Yes."

"Then are you telling me you're giving up?"

Groaning, I pushed myself upright, hating her for her prodding, and loving her for it too. "No."

"Good." Her gaze settled on the test in my hand. "When are you going to tell him?"

"Now," I said with a deep sigh. Mindful of the nausea, I scooted to the edge of the bed and swung my legs over. "Assuming he will actually listen, I'm going to tell him now."

Well, as soon as I got the strength in my legs to go knock on his hotel room door. I felt weak, numb, and dizzy, and not just a little bit scared. My hand crept over to rest on my belly for the millionth time. *I'm going to be a mommy*. Would I be a good one?

"Can I give you some advice?" Astrid asked, her tone full of the sort of quiet seriousness that put me on edge because it usually meant she intended to tell me something I didn't want to hear, but I nodded for her to go on just the same. "You're only a few weeks along. Anything can happen." Her lips twisted in a painful smile. "You've got a couple of months before you know this is the real deal, so take a moment to think about it, about how you feel and what it means to both of you, before you tell him. Okay?"

"Okay." I nodded.

She was trying to protect me, prepare me in case this pregnancy ended badly. 'Cause no matter how much you wanted it to, sometimes things just didn't work out, as we'd discovered when she'd gone to the hospital, bleeding and in pain, and the doctor had talked to us about the realities of early-term miscarriage.

And maybe Lucas wouldn't want a baby, so was it fair to tell him something so life-altering when our relationship was pretty much over? If he'd moved on, would he want to know until I was certain that in a few months he'd need to be changing diapers and coughing up monthly support?

But I already knew how I felt about him and the

baby. I wanted them both in my life. Badly. It might not amount to marriage, but oh my God, I was going to have a *baby*! And no matter what had happened yesterday, or how things turned out in the future, I knew in my heart of hearts that Lucas deserved to know he was a daddy. Right now.

I guess she saw the decision in my eyes, because she gave my hand a squeeze while she puffed out a little resigned sigh. "Okay then. I'm going for a shower. Unless you want me around?"

"Thanks, but I think I need to do this alone."

She nodded. "And what are you going to do if *he's* not alone?" Her eyes narrowed as she glared at the door adjoining our rooms. No sound came from his side, but that didn't mean anything.

Cry, I felt like saying, but I put on my brave act instead. "I'll kick his sorry ass."

"That's my girl," Astrid said, and with a little kiss to my cheek, she headed for the washroom. Pausing at the doorway, she looked back. "Scream if you need help kicking some ass."

I laughed and once she'd shut the door, rose to

my feet. Right. Time to pay the piper. What was the worst that could happen? That he'd ignore my knocking again? Or open the door and slam it in my face? Either way, I had to try.

My bare feet padded softly on the carpeted floor as I steeled my nerves. One thing was for certain, even if this all worked out and we got back together, I wouldn't be able to wear that Steam Bunny costume for much longer. A baby bump wouldn't appear for a few months yet, but the idea of trying to struggle into that leather corset and tight bodice made me want to faint. My breasts seemed to have grown again overnight and swayed like udders when I walked. I felt more like Steam Cow today than Steam Bunny.

I giggled at my own silliness, bolstering my spirit with fake bravado as I knocked on Lucas's door. Sucking in a breath, I scrunched my toes into the carpet. This conversation needed to happen no matter how shaky and upset I felt. My breath caught as the knob turned. *Finally, he was going to speak to me.* Except it wasn't Lucas who stood before me in the gap between our rooms. Hyacinth paused there, eyeing me expectantly.

I froze. My heart pounded, struggling to keep blood rushing to my head as a sick, sick feeling of horror settled in my belly. I'd known it was possible he wasn't alone in his room, but I'd thought I'd made it more than clear she wasn't welcome anymore, especially not '*later*'. Yet, here she stood, wet hair plastered to her head, wearing the same robe as I had on—white terry cloth, with extra pockets and plushness, compliments of the Chicago Marriott.

"Good morning, Ms. Jackson," she said politely, squeezing out a couple of dimples that I wanted to smack right off her face. "Can I help you with anything?" She looked at me all perky and bright-eyed, as if there was nothing at all wrong with standing there, freshly washed and probably nude beneath that robe, in my man's room.

I managed to somehow find my voice, but it came out as a strangled whisper. "Lucas...?"

"He's still in the shower." She glanced over her

shoulder toward the bathroom, allowing me a view of the room and the bottle of wine uncorked on the table with two glasses tipped on their sides, the ice bucket, also tipped over, its contents long since melted, and sketch pads strewn across the floor, like someone had been busy drawing, and, and…oh God, and bits of her clothes were draped haphazardly over the furniture. Her bra actually hung from a lamp. *It freakin' hung from a lamp!*

I shut my eyes and backed away, unable to deal with the sight before me. It was one thing to suspect, but to see it, to *know*…the sickness in my belly roiled as it clenched with pain. He'd left yesterday, angry and frustrated. Telling me he didn't fucking care what the hell I did anymore. But he'd said he *loved* me. That he loved *me*. Now I knew he'd played me for a bigger fool than I'd ever thought possible.

"He'll be done any minute," Hyacinth said. "You're welcome to come in and—hey, are you okay?"

Cramped over, I made it back to my bed, nausea

rising like a brackish wave. "Just close the fucking door and leave," I snarled. The last thing I needed to see was her gloating, dimpled smile while I cried.

I couldn't hold my tears inside. I just couldn't. They ran down my cheeks as I rolled onto my side and buried my face in my pillow. My heart pounded painfully in my chest as it shattered into pieces. Oh God. I was pregnant. And the father was the King of All Assholes. Yes, I'd hurt him by not saying yes when he'd asked me to marry him. But to play with me so cruelly—it was unforgivable. He was just like my father after all. Making a promise then screwing off when the going got tough. And to think I'd *almost* fallen for it. Had he *ever* truly loved me?

"Casey?" Lucas called out, his deep voice full of concern. The springs creaked as he sat down on my bed, the scent of bergamot soap fresh from his shower enveloping me like a cruel joke. "What's wrong?"

Ha! As if he didn't know.

His hand gently caressed my back and shoulders.

Stroking, soothing. Except I didn't want to be soothed. I wanted him to die. "Don't…f-fucking…t-touch me." I sobbed. I tried to roll away and shake him off, but he followed me, his grip tightening.

"Are you sick? Does something hurt?" He sounded distraught. "Casey, baby?"

Casey, baby?

Seriously? He had the nerve to insult me with endearments when he'd just spent the night with someone else? Not only was Lucas the King of All Assholes, he was the World's Biggest Idiot. If I'd had the strength, I'd have crowned him with the nearest table lamp. Instead, I clutched my belly and moaned as nausea made the room spin. Of all the humiliating things to happen, now I might just puke. And Astrid was in the bathroom, the hiss of the shower loud and clear despite my sniffling. I couldn't even escape to worship the porcelain throne.

"What happened?" Lucas asked, his snappish tone a mixture of bewilderment, concern and impatience, but that wasn't directed at me, that was at *her*, because for some reason Hyacinth still invaded the room. Her light footfalls padded close to the bed as she watched while I blubbered and turned six shades of green.

"I don't know." She sounded anxious. "I'm very sorry, Mr. Haskell. I was hanging up my clothes to dry, trying to clean up the mess I made. I heard a knock on the door. So I answered, like you'd asked me to. But when I told her you were still in the shower, she went really pale and...oh."

Oh?

"Oh!" she said again, more forcefully as if she'd just realized something important. "Oh, God. I think that maybe she...ah, she might have thought that, um.... You know, I think that maybe I should just leave."

Finally! Don't let the door hit you on the way out, you little man-stealing slut!

Lucas didn't answer her. His hand stilled its soothing rhythm and jerked away from me, his body suddenly tense.

Swallowing the sickness as the room spun, I

slowly rolled until I could see him. His damp hair stuck to his face and neck, curling where it dried. He wore only boxers, his naked chest beautiful in the morning light. The Celtic love knots tattooed across his pecs seemed to ripple beneath his crisp dark hairs as his breath became ragged. Clutched in his fingers were the pregnancy tests I'd left on my bedside table.

His gaze slid to mine, full of the question in his hands, his jaw flexing tight.

Time slowed as I struggled to sit up, to face this moment head on.

"Is this why you're so upset?" he whispered, the pulse at his neck beating hard.

"No," I shook my head, then immediately wished I hadn't as my belly spasmed.

Hyacinth, for all her intentions of leaving, still stood by the door, her mouth hanging open as she witnessed my moment of reckoning as if it were the penultimate scene of a favorite daytime Soap. Jesus, of all the stupid girls in the world Lucas could go for. It was more than humiliating. It was an insult to everything we'd ever been to each other. And it was too much.

"Why the hell did you have to fuck *her*?" I spat out, pointing at the 'her' in question with a stab of my finger.

And though I tried to turn my head, to stop the inevitable with my hand, I heaved a volley of nasty, greenish vomit, straight down that sexy chest of his and onto his traitorous lap. rt chapter six text here. Insert chapter six text here.

Call Me Baby, Maybe

I'M PRETTY SURE that of all the outbursts in my life, of all the things I'd said in the past and would ever say in the future, the words *"Why the hell did you have to fuck her?"* ranked in the top ten worst moments of my life, destined to haunt me forever.

The scene played out in my mind as I lay on my bed, tormenting me over and over again with the whiney, petty, jealous screech in my voice and the way Hyacinth's eyes had practically bugged right out of her head as she'd looked at Lucas, her face burning, and then finally—*finally*—bolted from the room, gagging.

The look in *his* eyes as he'd stared at me, first in shock at the volley of sick-goo, then in disappointment, then with an angry glare as Astrid had raced from the bathroom like a freakin' Norse Valkyrie wrapped in a towel, wet hair steaming, to literally kick him out of the room—yeah, that would stay with me forever too.

"I told him not to make you cry," Astrid said with a satisfied smile, which didn't quite ease the worry from her eyes.

Sitting beside me on the bed, she pressed a cool cloth to my forehead again. Coupled with the hot beanbag soothing my aching belly as I lay tucked under soft, clean covers, my body propped up by a pile of downy pillows, I had finally calmed down. Astrid was insisting on treating me like a delicate piece of porcelain in imminent danger of breaking. She'd even stayed in the bathroom while I'd cleaned myself up and showered, afraid I might faint or something. And maybe she was right. I felt fragile and thin, like I'd been stretched too far, and

I'd be happy if I never had to move a muscle again.

But I managed a giggle, despite my miserable state. "Where the hell did you learn to kick ass like that?"

"Hey. I live in New York. Self-defense classes, baby." She lifted her arm and hiked up the sleeve of her t-shirt, pumping up her skinny bicep for me to see. "I am woman, hear me roar."

I laughed loud at her girl-power antics and more of the ache eased.

"Awesome job with the puking, though," she said. "Ker-splat! Right on his cheating dick. Casey, my girl. You rock."

"I agree," Lucas said, his deep voice carrying across the room. "She does rock."

He stood in the arch of our adjoining doorway, fresh from his second shower of the morning. Dressed in black skinny jeans that hugged his hips and thighs just right, a pair of Doc Marten boots, and a black *Steam Bunny* t-shirt, which showed off his lean arm muscles, he looked mouth-wateringly, heart-achingly, gorgeous. Especially with his lopsided smile and that soft—dare I say tender?—glow in his ice blue eyes.

"But maybe go easy on the O.J. next time," he added with a wink.

"Ugh," Astrid grimaced as she looked at me. "Sorry, babe. I should have locked that door. Do you want me to kick him out again?"

"No," I said as he casually walked into the room ignoring Astrid, his gaze only for me.

My heartbeat thundered. I hadn't been sure if I ever wanted to see him again after what I'd seen in his room, but now that he was here, I was anxious to speak with him. There were a few things we needed to discuss.

I caught Astrid's hand in mine. "Can you give us a minute alone, please?"

She looked like she'd rather walk on hot coals, but she nodded just the same. "Okay, but I won't be far if you need me."

Pressing a little kiss to my forehead, she headed for the door, but paused by Lucas where he leaned against the breakfast bar gazing at me, arms crossed over the large sketchbook he carried.

"How's it feel to have your ass handed to you by a girl?" she asked him sweetly.

He smiled. "Sore."

"Good," she growled. "Next time, I'm using stilettos. Do *not* upset her again." She wagged her finger in his face. "Casey and the baby need to rest."

"Yes, ma'am," he agreed, giving her a little salute.

"Promise me, Lucas," she insisted.

"*Astrid*," I snapped. I could fight my own battles. "Just leave it."

"Fine," she said throwing her hands up in a gesture of defeat. "But I'm only a text away."

The door closed behind her, leaving the room full of silence.

Lucas glanced at the mostly untouched tray of breakfast beside him on the counter. "I guess they forgot the Ginger Ale, but at least they got the flowers right." He picked one of the chocolate roses from the bouquet and brought it to his nose to sniff.

A smile lifted the corners of his sculpted lips as he sauntered towards me.

"Those are from you?" I asked.

He paused mid-stride. His brows lowered as his gaze narrowed on me. "You were expecting someone else to send you breakfast and flowers?"

Huh. How about that. I could still make the dickhead jealous. Taking the cloth from my brow, I tossed it onto the side table, resisting the urge to run into his arms wielding a sharp knife.

I hadn't expected him to be nice right now. I wasn't certain what I'd expected from him except down-on-his-knees-begging-me-to-forgive-him-guilt, but nice? Definitely not, and my bruised heart couldn't quite make sense of what it meant.

Calm down, I reminded myself, taking a deep breath. *Give him a chance to explain.*

I'd had some time to think while I'd been in the shower. What he'd done was unforgivable, but if I wanted a civil relationship with Lucas for the baby's sake, which I did, even if he was, as Astrid had said, "a cheating bastard who needed his dick chopped off", then I needed to set the bar higher and bite down on the urge to act like Lorena Bobbitt.

I managed a cool smile. "We thought it might have been Astrid's hot date from last night."

"Couldn't have been that hot if she's all nasty and cranky this morning," he muttered as he walked over to where I lay in my bed. "Guy needs to learn how to take care of his woman."

"*What?* Oh, really. And I suppose you—"

"Do you think the baby likes chocolate?" he asked, tapping the rose thoughtfully against his lips.

"I-I don't know."

Breaking off a petal, he bent down and popped it into my mouth. His fingers slid lazily where they touched my bottom lip.

"Sweet," he murmured as something hot flickered in his eyes.

"Mumph," I agreed, alarmed at how good the chocolate tasted as it melted in my mouth and how erotic the touch of his fingers on my lips had been. I really, really shouldn't have feelings like that for a man who'd just ripped my heart into pieces, but my body had always been a wanton fool where Lucas was concerned.

He watched me chew and swallow, his eyes hungrily tracing the path my tongue made as I licked my lips clean of the sticky sweet goodness.

"I'm glad you're feeling better," he murmured. "You've got some color back in your beautiful face. More?" he asked offering me another petal.

"Not yet. Better not push it with the food, you know?"

"Definitely," he said with a tight smile. "You scared the shit out of me this morning."

"*I* scared the shit out of *you*?"

"Hell, yeah. I thought you were dying or something."

I was. I'd been a drowning woman with no one to throw me a lifeline. Luckily, I was strong enough to swim to the surface alone.

"You know," he said with a soft smile on his lips as he gazed down at me. "That first day we met, when you walked into my studio looking like

Marilyn Monroe, except better?"

"*Marilyn Monroe?* Are you serious? I'm not nearly as pretty. And my hair's strawberry, not peroxide blond."

I touched my untamed hair self-consciously as a blush crept over my skin. I'd brushed my teeth and ran a comb through my long curls, but without any make-up on, I must have looked like hell. Not that I cared what Lucas thought, but still, it was always better not to appear like you belonged on *PeopleofWalmart.com*.

"Well, I guess I like strawberry," he said, his smile deepening. "Because I've never gotten you out of my mind since."

My pulse raced at the warmth in his eyes and voice. Luckily, it was just my body's newfound radar for sensing bullshit blaring a warning.

"Yeah, right," I said not buying a word of it. "You just like my boobs." Flattery was a nice try, but he needed to do *waaay* better than a bit of sweet-talking to make up for what he'd done. If he ever could.

"Yeah." He chuckled. "I do." His gaze settled on my chest as if he were Superman trying to see through my t-shirt with x-ray vision. "But it's more than that. It's always been more than that." His expression turned serious, the pain of the past few weeks leaking through into his eyes. "Why do you think I went a bit crazy when you said you didn't want to get married? Losing you felt like I'd lost a part of me."

"So, you decided to fuck the first piece of ass you ran into last night?" My heart squeezed tight at the anguish in his gaze, but it wasn't anything close to the raw pain I felt.

He shook his head. "That's not what happened, Casey." Putting the sketchbook on the bedside table, he raked his fingers through his hair.

"She was in your room, Lucas. Naked. I'm *not* blind."

"She wasn't naked. She was wearing a robe."

"*Like it matters.*" Jesus Fucking Christ. That knife might come in handy after all.

"Do you really think I'd tell you I love you and

then fuck somebody else?" he snapped.

"It happens all the time," I whispered, tears prickling my eyes again.

He closed his own, his brow tightening. "Listen," he said after a moment. He wiped his hand over his face. "I know you're upset and hurting right now—
"

"You think?"

. "Fuck…" he whispered. Rolling his shoulders, he forced himself to relax as he stared down at me. A heavy sigh passed over his lips, his tired gaze searching mine, his features softening. "I don't want to argue with you, Casey. I just want to make it better again. Can I sit down?"

Make it better? Nothing would ever make my heart feel better again. But I patted the covers beside me and shifted over a little, giving him some room.

A relieved smile tipped his lips. "Thank you."

Putting the rose between his teeth like a tango dancer, he pulled a tiny bottle of massage oil out of his back pocket and placed it on top of the sketchbook.

Massage oil? Was he kidding? "Um…Lucas?"

"Yeah?" he mumbled around the rose as he sat down on the edge of the bed.

"What about Hyacinth?"

It killed me to say her name. Seriously, it *killed* me to contemplate her existence. But I needed to know what she meant to him.

Silence stretched while he undid his boots and kicked them onto the floor. Then, taking the rose from his mouth, he flashed his pearly whites. "Don't worry," he said. "I talked to her and she's cool with everything." Leaning sideways, he tucked the flower in the open V-neck of my shirt, nestling it snug against my warm skin. "We don't need all these covers, do we? It must be like a furnace under there."

He started to pull the covers off, but I stilled him with my hand on his wrist.

"Stop," I commanded, feeling all sorts of different kinds of heat rising inside. "It might be cool with her if you fool around with other people, but it's definitely *not* cool with me," I said as cool and calm as possible, which wasn't cool and calm at all, but more like a hot snarl. "Are you fucking her?"

"No," he said without hesitation.

"Or anyone else?"

"No." Now he sounded annoyed. His brow furrowed. "Why would I?"

Why indeed? Like he didn't know he was a sex-god incarnate with women drooling at his heels. "Good," I said, but doubt clung.

Could I trust it? Could I trust him? I wished with all my heart that his words were real, yet I couldn't unsee what I'd seen, no matter how much he tried to smooth things over.

"But if you're only here to play games with me, then you'd better just leave," I warned.

"Okay," he agreed after a pause, studying me with that penetrating gaze of his. "No games."

"Thank you," I said, watching him carefully. "No games."

Leaving the covers where they were, he lay back

against the mountain of pillows, propped his hands behind his head and crossed his ankles so that the sexy length of him stretched out beside me. Thankfully the bed was a double, because the heat in the room had become stifling. It could have been all the covers, but I suspected it was the ridiculous ability he had to set fire to my blood, no matter how hurt or mad I felt, thanks to that devastating combination of bergamot and *him*.

"But I should probably point out," he said with a meaningful glance at my chest, "that rose is going to melt chocolate all over you soon, and I can't be held responsible for what will happen when I clean it up. With my tongue."

"You are *such* an asshole." Couldn't he respect my pain, not even a little? Snatching the rose from between my breasts, I tossed it at him in disgust. "Fine. Be a dick. Play stupid games if you want to. I'm out of here."

I tossed the beanbag aside and kicked off the covers, freeing myself from the heat, but he pinned me to the mattress with a steely arm draped across my middle.

"No, you're not," he said, his voice full of preternatural calm. "You're going to rest in bed today and let me pamper you."

Okay, he really was fucked in the head. "Why the hell would I ever do that?"

"Because as much as you love to be all prickly and in control, you're going to have to bend on this one and listen to me for a change. There's a baby to think of now."

Yes. There was. And he was *not* going to control me with it. "For God's sake. I'm not an invalid," I snapped, trying to push him away. "I'm just pregnant."

"*Just* pregnant?" His voice rose. "*Just?*" His eyes flashed as he pulled me close to his side, the fierce strength and heat of him scorching my skin. "How can you think of this as *just* a pregnancy? That little baby is the most important thing in the world right now. And despite everything that's happened, it was created out of love. So be angry with me if you want to, I don't fucking care. But for

Christ's sake, don't you *ever* take it out on the baby."

Whoa. Whoa, whoa, whoa, whoa, *whoa!* Hold on now. I wasn't taking anything out on the baby. Was I? But his nostrils flared, his jaw tight, so maybe he truly thought I was.

"Lucas," I began. "I don't think—"

"Bullshit," he snapped. "All you do is think. You, think and think and think all the god-damned time. But did you ever stop to consider that what you think might be wrong?"

"Well, I know I'm not perfect, but—"

"Exactly, *but*. There's always a '*but*' with you, 'cause in your mind you can never make a mistake."

"Ah...am I missing something here?" I mean, wasn't I supposed to be upset with him? He was the one who'd fucked someone else out of spite last night. Right? Why was he so upset with me?

He rolled his eyes and shook his head. "Just shut up and roll over so I can give you a massage."

What? How was I supposed to relax and enjoy that with him acting so freakin' pissed?

"I really don't think that's a good idea," I said.

I mean, ick factor aside with having his traitorous fingers work their magic on me, I wore only skimpy pink panties and a loose white shirt, and his massages were not just good, they were sensually, erotically, amazingly good. He might think I was born yesterday, but I could see right through this little ploy with the chocolate roses and the nicey-niceness and I had no intention of sleeping with him ever again.

"Casey, I'm not trying to seduce you. I just want you to relax."

Right. If I had a penny for every guy who'd ever said that in the history of guys, I'd be a zillionaire able to hire a whole legion of man-slaves to massage me whenever I wished.

"You can keep your clothes on," he insisted, and to his credit his gaze stayed locked on mine instead of glancing at the clothes, or lack thereof, in question. "I won't do anything you don't want me to do. Scout's honor." He raised his hand in the classic two-finger salute.

"Lucas," I said, struggling to keep my voice even as the urge to laugh built. "You were *never* in Boy Scouts."

He grinned. "Then, I guess you'll just have to trust me."

Ha! I sucked in a sharp breath. Could I do that ever again? Was this a test of my virtue or his?

"Fine," I blurted out, raising my chin at the dare in his eyes. "Do your worst." *Asshole.*

It was all still a game to him, of course, but my lower back ached like Hyacinth had stuck pins in a voodoo doll of me, and after all the stress of the last three weeks and that delicious scent of his confounding my defenses with memories of closeness, I was hard pressed to resist what he offered. Seriously, I had to find a way to bottle that smell. Eau de Studly Manliness. I'd make a mint.

Chucking some of the pillows on the floor, I gingerly rolled onto my belly, mindful of my sore breasts.

"Good," he said, kneeling beside me on the bed. "Now turn off whatever crazy crap thinking goes through your head and just feel."

Was he kidding? All I'd been doing was feeling. Mostly like shit, but I couldn't deny how good his palms felt, radiating warmth through my thin shirt as his hands pressed against the tight muscles of my back. A soft little moan escaped me as he worked his fingers on a particularly sensitive spot that burned from all the hours yesterday trapped in that stupid costume.

"That's right. Just relax," he murmured. "Getting so worked up all the time isn't good for you or the baby."

Ah, yes. The baby. I wasn't going to survive the next nine months with sanity intact if everyone kept treating me like I couldn't take care of myself. But he'd surprised me with his protectiveness over what some men might think of as a problem. Especially now.

"So…" I said turning onto my side and looking up at him. "So, you're, um, fine with this then?" Not that it would change anything whether he was or wasn't. I could raise a child on my own. But still…I placed my hand on the flat of my belly.

"You know, Casey. I should be seriously pissed you'd even ask that." And his stubbled jaw did clench tight. "But as you're a bit of an emotional train wreck right now, I'll explain this as plainly as I can, so we don't have any more misunderstandings." Placing his big hand over top of my small one, he entwined our fingers and looked me deep in the eyes. "This baby, growing right in here, is the best news I've had. Ever. I can't wait to meet him or her. So yes, I'm more than fine with this. I love this." He gave my fingers a tight squeeze.

Oh, shit. *Here comes the water works.* I guess there must have been a part of me that'd really cared what he thought, because at the warm look in his eyes and the way they glistened softly, relief shot through me and the room misted.

"You love the baby?" I whispered.

"Yeah, I do," he said and bent down to place a little kiss upon our joined hands covering my belly. "Hey now, no crying. Or Astrid will kick my ass so hard I'll be shitting through my teeth."

"Ah, God." I laughed despite myself, my tears dissolving into hiccupy sniffles. I wiped my cheeks with my palms and shook my head at how easily I seemed to cry at everything these days. Even a Puppy Chow commercial I'd seen last night on TV had set me off. "I am such a freakin' mess."

"Yeah, you are." His lips brushed my forehead in a tender kiss that touched deep into my wounded heart. "Now settle back down so I can help you relax."

Sadness ached in my chest as I followed his instruction. We could have been a nice family. Living together, loving together, watching our baby grow. Maybe in a bit of time we could even have gotten married. Hadn't I changed my 'no' to a 'maybe'? Why hadn't that been good enough for him? Why, for God's sake, had he ruined everything by sleeping with stupid Hyacinth? I was certain he'd done so, despite his claims.

He'd been angry with me. Frustrated and hurt. She'd been after him all day. If she'd come to his room while he was so upset and thrown herself at him? Especially if he'd had a couple of drinks? What guy could resist temptation like that? Lucas wasn't Superman.

Just like I wasn't Lois Lane.

We were real people with real troubles. Real fears. Real dreams.

He'd said he loved me. And I'd said I loved him.

Then why had I hurt him again and again by refusing to marry him?

I swallowed hard as his hands slid over my back, his strong fingers working the resistance from my tight muscles.

Had he *ever* given me reason to doubt his word until now?

I played the scene over again, but try as I might, I couldn't recall what Hyacinth had said before racing from his room this morning. All I could see was her standing there in that robe and the wounded look in his eyes.

He'd broken my heart. Had I broken his too?

"You're getting tense again," he murmured.

"Relax, Casey." Strong and warm, his fingers smoothed over my neck and down the back of my arms.

"I'm trying to," I whispered. Tears gathered, threatening to leak onto the pillow.

So, what if we'd fucked things up. Was the hurt we'd caused each other enough to stand in the way of a lifetime of happiness? A lot of years together as parents lay ahead of us. Maybe in time we could rebuild some trust. Maybe in time it would be the start of something new.

Maybe.

So many maybes. Too many maybes. I let them wash over me as gently, yet firmly, he repeated the motion of his hands up and down my back and spine, over my shoulders and arms, soothing me until tears had been forgotten and the only thing in my mind was how incredibly good and warm he made me feel.

"Promise me one thing?" I murmured after some time.

"Mmm?"

"Don't ever stop what you're doing right now with your hands."

He gave a throaty chuckle. "You like my distraction?"

"Oh, God." I bit my lip as my wounded heart faltered and a giggle escaped. "I love your distraction."

"Good."

I smiled at the satisfaction and pleasure in his voice.

"I'm going to move under your shirt now. Okay?" he asked.

"Okay," I whispered, ready for more.

Cool air wafted across the skin of my back as he lifted the hem of my shirt and pushed it up to my shoulders. His fingers trailed down my naked spine, causing me to shiver.

"So soft," he whispered. "Absolutely beautiful."

My nipples tightened, pressing hard against the bed. My aching breasts wanted to have their turn at a massage too. Would I go for it if he asked me to roll over? Would I be strong enough to say no?

"You're thinking again, Casey," he said. The cap of the massage oil popped open and his hands slid quickly together as he warmed the lavender-scented liquid. "The only thing you need to do is feel."

He touched my skin, his strong hands caressing and relaxing me, the rhythmic movement erotic yet soothing until, limp and senseless, despite the hungry ache throbbing between my thighs, I no longer thought of anything at all.

****

I awoke with a start sometime later to the kiss of sunlight upon my cheek. Through a crack in the heavy chocolate brown curtains pulled closed against the day, rays of light peeked, falling across the head of my bed, tickling my skin with warm, playful fingers. I smiled and shifted out of reach. The sunlight danced across my pillow, trying to catch up.

Run, run, as fast as you can, you'll never catch me, I'm…I'm late for the convention. I had to be. That light was too bright for morning. What the heck time was it?

The alarm clock by Astrid's bed showed almost one p.m.

Almost one? Crap, I'd slept the morning away. When had I ever done that?

With a groan and a stretch, I rolled over beneath the cozy pile of covers and discovered two things: Lucas was nowhere to be seen in the room and my clothes were still on. Both of which should not have filled me with disappointment, but they did.

He'd caressed my body, massaging and kneading my muscles until I'd been a boneless ragdoll, limp with pleasure and seriously wet between my legs. He could have had me any way he wanted, and I'd never have resisted. Despite my earlier ranting about not sleeping with him again, I'd been so turned on, I hadn't cared about anything except the amazing way he made me feel deep, deep inside. Cherished. Adored. Loved? I'd been putty in his hands, soft and willing, and maybe I'd even begged. But true to his word, he'd not seduced me. He'd turned me into a puddle of desire and then left with a soft kiss on my cheek and the whispered wishes by my ear to have a good sleep.

What the hell was I supposed to make of that?

Had he left me alone because he'd only been caring for the baby's sake? Was it a sign he wasn't interested in that kind of a relationship with me anymore? Did the hurt between us go just too deep?

I couldn't deny that despite the hurt, I would have slept easier if he'd wrapped me in his warm, strong arms and I'd woken to see his gorgeous face like I always used to. My bruised heart would take more than a massage and decent sleep to mend, but my body felt relaxed, my mind refreshed, and joy of joys, no trace of nausea lingered to torment me.

My stomach growled, reminding me I'd only had a sliver of chocolate for breakfast. "Hello, Baby Bunny." I slid my hand over my belly, smiling. "Hungry, are you?"

Sitting up to go see what I could arrange from room service, I glanced at the night table and found a plate had been left there with a couple of chocolate drizzled croissants and a can of Ginger Ale, all perched atop the sketchbook Lucas had left behind.

Huh. Maybe it hadn't been the sunlight kissing my cheek that had woken me up after all. The can was opened and fizzing with a straw poking out. Someone had recently been in my room. Grinning, I reached for the plate, disturbing a note and three little white cards, which had been propped up for me to read.

Eat Me.

Drink Me.

Read Me.

Awwww. Now this…*this* was the Lucas I'd fallen in love with. The man with the brilliant mind who knew how to make me smile.

I broke off a piece of croissant and hungrily popped it in my mouth, the sweet, buttery pastry so fresh it practically melted on my tongue. Quickly polishing off the rest, I placed the empty plate beside me on the bed. Then, taking a sip of Ginger Ale, I read the note:

Super sexy man-beast

~~The Asshole~~ took your phone so I couldn't bug you. Like I don't know you need to sleep!!!?

I'm taking care of everything downstairs for you. So don't worry. Stay in bed and rest.

Love ya, chickie

XO ~~Astrid~~ **Ass-turd**

I laughed hard, shaking my head. Lucas must have gotten hold of the note after Astrid had left it and added his own two cents. *Super sexy man-beast.* God, he was cruising for another ass kicking when she found out.

Hunger temporarily sated, I dragged the sketchbook over, settling myself against the pillows for a good read. Lucas literally owned hundreds of these kinds of drawing books, so what was special about this one?

The book rested heavy against my legs, the hard black cover stained like it had been on the receiving end of a spill. It wasn't like Lucas to be clumsy. He took care of things. I was the messy one, cluttering up the loft we'd shared with all my "junk," as he called it. Maybe I'd cluttered up his life with it too.

I flipped through the first few pages of white vellum, glancing at the drawings, and had the eerie sensation of tumbling down a rabbit hole.

Most of them were of me. Little rough sketches where he'd caught me unawares, like when I sat at our kitchen table working on my laptop, my curly hair long and loose. In another, he'd posed me as a curvy 1940's pin-up girl, coiling my hair into a classic Monroe-do. Huh. Maybe I did look a bit like her. In many I was dressed as Steam Bunny, different character studies and costume ideas. The latest version had me cinched tight by that corset, my breasts full and heavy, a look of sadness in my eyes as I smiled at the crowd. When had he drawn that? Yesterday at the signing? There'd been no other time.

Frowning, I rifled through a stack of loose water-stained pages bound together with a clip. Ah, this was the new story he'd been working on. Scribbled notes and quick story panels jotted down with feverish intensity, judging by the hasty strokes. Apparently, the nefarious Dr. Vascular had broken into his lab again and created a new evil minion for Steam Bunny to fight, a sleek little minx called Ninja Kitten.

And there they were, the sketches he'd said he done of Hyacinth. She'd posed for him, all right. Fully clothed, doing what were quite incredible karate moves, with no indication in his pencil work of any attraction to her lithe figure. He'd enjoyed her athleticism, that was clear in the dynamic lines, but his pencil had not lingered on her breasts, caressing them to make them fuller, or added any luster to her lips. Whereas I…a hot blush crept over my skin as I stared at the next page. Even wrinkled and water stained, the erotic image remained clear.

He'd drawn me lounging naked on my side, hair a riot of long flowing curls, my full lips parted in a soft smile as I caressed my rounded, distended belly, my breasts heavy and nipples hard as if begging to be kissed. Heat spiked as my body awakened to the truth in that picture. This was how Lucas imagined me—sensual and stimulating, luscious and beautiful…and pregnant with his child.

"Oh shit. Shit, shit, shit," I hissed and closed the sketchbook with a snap.

A groan escaped as I cradled my head in my hands. I had no idea what had happened this morning in his room with Hyacinth, but I knew I'd been a stupid, idiotic, fool. He must have drawn that picture before I'd told him about the baby. It was on the same paper he'd used for his drawings of Hyacinth. Which meant he'd been thinking of me all along, even while he'd been working with her, suspecting I might be pregnant and imagining how sexy I'd look if it were true.

Were those the actions of a cheating asshole? A God-damned-prick-bastard-jerk who deserved to die? My heart answered with a resounding *"NO."*

Every horrible name I'd ever called him flew through my mind like nasty, stinging barbs. Oh, what a bitch I'd been. A horrible jealous bitch. So why hadn't he told me the truth? Or had he and I just hadn't listened?

That's not what happened, Casey. His words echoed in my mind. *Do you really think I'd tell you I love you and then fuck somebody else?*

Apparently, I had.

Panicked, I kicked off the covers and hurried to the bathroom. I needed to get dressed, find him and apologize. I needed to—

A soft knock sounded on the door to my suite. Oh, thank God! Racing across the room, I opened the door in a hurry.

"Lucas," I said, breathless.

But standing on the other side, for the second unexpected time today, was Hyacinth.

Ninja Kitten

OH, GOD. TALK about awkward.

"Ah…sorry," I stammered, my face heating as I took a step backward from the door into my room. "I thought that you were, um… him."

"It's okay," Hyacinth said, without any trace of a dimple in sight. "I just wanted to…um, to, um…your shoes came from the Little Miss Kick-Ass vendor. So, I wanted to bring them up to you."

She thrust the box she held in her hands at me.

"Oh...um, thank you," I said taking the glossy black carton.

Her black, shoulder-length hair fell about her face like a curtain as she avoided my eyes. She was dressed for work, the *Steam Bunny* t-shirt and black jeans hugging her supple figure. Except today, her movements were less lithe and more rigid as she stood there waiting. She hadn't turned to go. Was I supposed to open the box?

Not knowing what else to do in the awkward silence, I undid the deep purple ribbon tied around the carton. Opening the lid, I peeked in the box and sighed. "Ah, my lovelies. Gorgeous, yes?" I lifted one of the leather stilettos I'd ordered, admiring the sexy ribbon tied up the heel that fastened like a corset. "Do you like shoes?"

She stared at me, her expression incredulous.

"I'm sorry," I whispered. Putting the shoe back in the box, I placed it on my nearby bed. "I'm not trying to be insulting. It's just...I've not been myself lately." Putting a smile on my face, I smoothed my hair over my shoulders as I faced her. I might not like her, but if Lucas hadn't slept with her, then should I really treat her like a man-stealing bitch?

"Let me start again. Thank you for bringing the shoes. I'm glad you're here. I owe you an apology. No, make that more than one." I grimaced as I thought of how nasty I'd been towards her over the past couple of days. "I said some things this morning that were really, well, really…bad. I'm sorry for that."

Her gaze slipped from mine. "Don't be," she whispered. Her expression twisted, looking for all the world like she might cry. "I'm the one who should be apologizing."

Oh. This was bad. My stomach tightened. Whatever Lucas had told her to smooth things over, she was definitely not "cool with everything" as he'd said.

"Okay," I said with a nod. Clearly she needed to talk. I wasn't certain I wanted to hear what she had to say, but I couldn't leave her standing stock-still in the doorway looking like hell warmed over. "Why don't you come in?" I offered, ushering her inside. I gestured at the breakfast bar and stools as I closed the door. "I can make some coffee."

She shook her head and remained standing. "I just wanted you to know that nothing happened. Lucas wouldn't…he didn't want to—to sleep. With me."

Her gaze flicked over me, pausing briefly on my bare legs and I realized I was still half-naked in my skimpy pink panties and loose white t-shirt. Grabbing a blanket from my bed, I wrapped it around me as understanding settled, unpleasant but not unexpected.

"But you wanted to sleep with him?" I prodded.

She nodded, her fists clenching at her sides. "He invited me to his room this morning. To be his model again. I thought he wanted something more. Why else would he have a bottle of wine open at that time of day?"

Oh fuck. I shook my head. "You don't have to do this," I said. I didn't want to hear any more. I could imagine it quite well myself. I was pretty sure I already had. "It's okay."

"No. It's not," she snapped. "I'm not a home-wrecker." Her eyes blazed as they found mine. "I thought you were done with him. I mean, you have separate rooms, right? And you've been arguing. A lot." She started pacing a little path between the door and my bed. "I know how things went at the drawing session, but I didn't want to believe it. And after what the guys in security said they saw on the balcony—"

"What?"

A blush crept over her cheeks. "It was apparently quite hot. Oh, don't worry," she said, her face pulling into a lopsided grin. "Happens all the time there. They call it the Fuck-Me Lounge."

"I'm going to kill Lucas," I whispered, squeezing my eyes shut tight. Cameras. Fuck. I liked people watching, *but not the whole freakin' world.*

"Well, yeah," said Hyacinth. "See? I know he left all angry, so I thought that was it. You were really done. But you aren't though, are you? You're having a baby."

"If I don't die from embarrassment first." I covered my face with my hands. I could just see that sex tape hitting the internet Tommy Lee and

Pamela Anderson style.

"Why? I think it's really hot. I wouldn't mind if I looked like you."

My hands slipped from my face at her tone and I caught an appreciative glimmer in her eyes as her gaze flicked over my body again. Okay, whoa. Wow. That kinda put a new spin on things. I backed up a step, pulling the blanket tighter around me. I wasn't up for any scissor-sister action.

"I can see why he's so stuck on you," she continued. "You're really lucky. Lucas is a great guy."

"Yeah, he is," I agreed. "Sometimes. But most of the time he's a clueless pain in the ass who has *no* idea what he does to women." A freakin' public sex tape. Every cock-loving person who watched it would be after his sexy ass now. Hells bells, I was really going to have to kill him.

A smile twisted her lips. "He made me so nervous, watching me while I posed for him, that I knocked the ice bucket onto his books this morning." She snickered. "And then, when I bent over to mop that up, I tripped and ended up with wine all over me. Why does he have to draw with his shirt off?"

I shook my head, thinking of his tight abs and gorgeous, lean muscles. "He let you off easy. He likes to draw butt naked."

Her eyes widened as she stopped dead in her tracks. "Oh, God."

"Yeah. It's a wonder we've ever gotten any work done."

She giggled, her shoulders relaxing as she plopped herself onto the edge of my bed and I could sort of see why Lucas liked her. She was bubbly, and cute, and honest to a fault. What a dickhead. He'd been playing with us both, just like I'd suspected from the start. Leading her on and enjoying it as she fawned over him, while I got spitting jealous.

"You know," I said thoughtfully. "I think someone's been a very naughty boy."

"Yeah," she said. "I think so too."

"How far did it go before he turned you down?"

Her face heated. "Well, I didn't get to kiss him, but I really wanted to."

"I see." I let out a breath I hadn't known I was holding. Okay, so he really hadn't touched her, but he still shouldn't have played such a manipulative game. Had he wanted me to think he'd slept with her this morning? "So...what do you think we should do about it?" I asked with a sly smile.

Her eyebrows rose. A sparkle lit her dark, almond-shaped eyes. "Well...those *are* killer shoes," she said, gesturing with a dimpled grin at the box she'd brought me. "Do you have a killer outfit to go with them?"

"Oh, hell yeah," I said, liking the angle of her thinking.

"Then why don't I help you get dressed while we talk?"

That Old Black Magic Called... Stilettos

I TIMED MY entrance at the convention perfectly, arriving right at the end of the autograph session and before the scheduled meeting with Lindstrom, three hours or so of free time in which to get Lucas alone and fuck some sense into him.

’Cause I’d figured out that’s what I’d been doing wrong all this time. Letting him call the shots about what we’d do and not do, then crying when it didn’t go my way. Stupid. If I wanted him to see things my way, I needed to take charge.

With Hyacinth's help, I'd dressed for success, putting on the brand new, never-before-seen kinky *Steam Bunny* number I'd brought with me for judging the character masquerade—and more specifically for tormenting the hell out of Lucas.

Sleeveless, jacketless, the black burlesque corset dress laced down my back, accenting my small waist and curvy figure as it hugged my ass in a sleek short skirt of heavy satin. Across my chest large brass gears molded my ample breasts like two metal bull's-eyes, while lace bows kissed my hips and clung low across the middle of my behind, draping like a tail.

Okay. Yeah, it was a bit over the top for daywear, or, well, anywhere, and it fit a bit tight on the chest, but no pain, no gain, right? It wouldn't be on for long if I had my way. I'd kept my curls long and loose the way Lucas liked best, pulling my hair back from my brow with a bunny-ear headband. My lips were glossy crimson red, my nails equally so, and my shoes…oh God, the new lovelies fit like a dream, making my legs seem longer and sleeker than they'd ever been.

Fingerless black fishnet gloves covered my hands. Stark against my pale skin and that sparkling diamond on my finger.

I felt more than a bit nervous about that. Marriage. I grimaced, my heart racing. But I'd made my choice and it was Lucas. If I loved him, and I did despite the fact he could be a giant asshole at times, then I needed to show him I meant business.

"I can't wait to see his face when he sees us." Hyacinth giggled as we pushed our way through the crowd toward the *Steam Bunny* booth. Not that we had to do much pushing. The crowd parted on its own as people turned to look at me, stopped talking, then erupted into loud whispers, which followed me like an excited wave.

"They've seen that sex tape, haven't they?" I whispered to Hyacinth, my face heating.

She shrugged. "They've probably just heard about it. Security'd get fired for doing that."

I raised my chin and kept on walking through the crowd. Well, whatever had been done couldn't be undone, and maybe I could use it to my advantage now. I smiled at all the sidelong, interested glances. *Hold onto your Lightsabers, kids. You ain't seen nothin' yet.* I was done with hiding away.

I spotted Astrid packing up equipment at the *Steam Bunny* booth. She chatted with the Bat Guy, still in costume at her side. He paused, eyes widening as he caught sight of me, his hands full of the laptop bag Astrid had given him to hold. Giving her a nudge, his lips spread into an appreciative smile.

Looking up to see what had caught his attention, she did a double take. "Casey?"

I shushed her with a finger to my lips and pointed at Lucas.

He was engrossed in signing some books for a couple of green-skinned, red-haired Orion slave girls from *Star Trek*. I crossed my arms, waiting to see how long it would take for him to notice me. True to his clueless-man self, he seemed oblivious to the change in the air as the conversation around him stopped. After hosting a morning seminar on Steampunk gizmos and gadgets, followed by three hours of pimping his books and signing autographs, he looked tired but otherwise his smile held, his pearly whites flashing wide at something one of the girls had said.

Their giggling smiles slipped as the Orion bimbos noticed me. Eyes widening, they moved to the side, giving me room to deal with Lucas.

I perched my hip on the table and leaned sideways toward him like a sultry pin-up doll. "Can I get your autograph, Mr. Haskell?" I asked, my voice husky with desire.

His smile froze as he glanced up at me, his gaze darting over the outfit I wore and getting stuck on my brass and satin-covered breasts jutting in front of his eyes.

"Sweet Jesus," he said swallowing hard. His tongue darted out to lick his lips.

I grinned, pleasure spiraling in my belly at the way his muscles tensed, his eyes darkening with arousal as they took in the view.

"Right here would be just fine," I teased, tracing my finger along the curve of my breasts where they peeked from the fitted cups. His eyes followed every inch of the movement as his nostrils flared, breathing in the vanilla spice perfume I'd sprayed on just for him. "But maybe you'd like me to pay first. Hum?" I whispered.

Bending closer, I lifted his chin with a manicured nail. I looked deep into his intense, sexy eyes, holding the heat in them for a moment. Then I grasped his face between my hands and kissed him for all I was worth.

I am yours, my heart cried out, beating an excited rhythm as my lips molded over his, *and you are mine*.

He growled low in answer. His hand grasped my bare shoulder, the other snagged in my hair as he pulled me closer, deepening the searing kiss.

Cheers and clapping pierced by wolf whistles erupted around us. I smiled inside, savoring his intoxicating taste as I branded him for everyone to see, reaffirming that he was mine and I was most definitely staying on as Steam Bunny. I wasn't going anywhere, not without him by my side.

"I'm giving you chocolate croissants for lunch every day from now on," he said sounding breathless as he came up for air.

"Oh baby," I said with a giggle, rubbing my thumb across the red lipstick smeared on his lips. "That's not all I like for lunch. We have some unfinished business."

I slid off the table. Reaching out to Hyacinth, who stood nearby grinning, I slipped my arm around her slim waist. She did the same, her hand grabbing my hip as she pulled me tight against her side.

"Jesus," Lucas said. He sat back in his chair, staring between the two of us as if waiting for the other shoe to drop. "So, what is this? A conspiracy?"

"Care to join us for a little fun?" I asked. Taking the little white card that she held in her hand, I tossed it onto the table for him to read.

Eat me.

His eyes narrowed, tiny spots of color heating his face. "What the hell are you doing, Casey?"

I looked at Hyacinth as she stroked my hip with the palm of her hand. It really did nothing for me, but the tense expression on Lucas's face was priceless. "I thought you'd like this," I said batting my eyes innocently at him. "Both of us, together at the same time. It's what you wanted, isn't it?"

His eyes darkened. "Okay, I get it. You're made your point. But Captain Kirk's nipples, Casey, do you have to do it in front of the crowd?"

"Well maybe it'll give them something to think about instead of that sex tape," I growled.

"Ah...you've heard about that already." He flicked an accusing glare at Hyacinth.

Laughing, she gave me a peck on the cheek as she slid her hand from my hip and turned her attention to her chiming phone. "Sorry Haskells, I gotta take this."

"Haskells?" Lucas's gaze snagged on my left hand and the diamond I wore.

"Casey." Astrid shrieked as she knocked me sideways, giving me a tight hug. Letting go, she glanced at Hyacinth with a raised brow, incredulous and curious.

"It's a long story," I said. "I'll explain later."

"I bet it's an interesting one." She levelled me with a hard stare. "What the hell are you doing out of bed?" Her hands fisted on her hips.

"Whoa, there, Little Miss Kick-ass," I said, holding up my hands in a mock attempt at protecting myself from her wrath. "I've had enough of being in bed. At least alone."

I smiled at Lucas, a thousand insecurities clawing my insides. Had I done the right thing after all by wearing that ring? "Come with me?" I asked.

I crooked my finger at him in a sexy beckon for him to follow, but he was already there, walking around the table, his intense gaze riveted on me.

"Yes, ma'am," he said. Catching my outstretched fingers in his, he brought my hand to his lips. He kissed the ring on my finger, causing a little zing of pleasure straight to my heart, and a few giggles from some nearby girls.

"Everything's ready upstairs," Hyacinth said. Finishing a text on her phone, she hit send. "Room 1501. Door is open for you. Key cards are on the table." She smiled. "I'll take care of the rest of this stuff." She gestured toward the camera equipment and swag accessories at our booth. "If you need anything else, just call."

"God, you're awesome," I said and gave her a quick hug. "Thank you, Hyacinth."

Lucas's thumb rubbed my palm, his fingers clutching mine. Anxious to be alone with him, I quickly led him through the churning crowd and out of the convention hall.

"Okay," he said as we hurried down a quiet corridor in search of the main elevator. "I'm never going to understand women." He shook his head. "You and Hyacinth are what? BFF's now? This morning you wanted to kill her."

"That's because you've been a bad boy," I murmured, wrapping my arm about his waist. The heat coming off him was incredible. "Leading her on and making me jealous. Can you blame me for thinking you fucked her?"

"Ah," he said as we stopped before the elevator, our reflections distorted in the polished brass doors. He pushed the arrow to go up and cupped my bare shoulders with his arm. "So, you've changed your mind about that, have you?"

I looked up at his face. "Why didn't you just tell me?"

His brows flicked. "I did." A shadow of sadness darkened his eyes. "There's this thing called trust in relationships, Casey. You've been hell-bent on me being an asshole for the past three weeks. You didn't want to believe me."

Ah. Right. Well, he had me there. I glanced away, ashamed that it was true.

He'd been acting like a prick out of spite for my rejection, but I'd been looking for every little excuse to turn him into a monster. It made it easier to run and hide, to justify my fear of trusting him. But I wasn't willing to hide anymore. Lucas was not like my father. He was not the sort of man to break his commitments on a selfish whim. And having seen what damage my panic had caused, I'd started a new list in my head called 'Reasons I Should Never Doubt Lucas', at the top of which was the wonderful fact that despite my prickly nature, he loved me.

There were always going to be times in our life when we'd be apart both physically and emotionally, but I had to have faith that if he gave me his word, his heart, and his hand in marriage, it was a gift to be cherished, not squandered. Unfortunately, our antics over the past three weeks had done a good job of bruising it.

As the elevator doors opened with a 'bing', he guided me inside. Finger hovering over the panel of buttons, he raised a brow at me. "I'm guessing floor fifteen?" he asked. "That was the room level she said, right?"

I smiled. He never missed a beat. "Yes."

He nodded with a sparkle in his eye. "Top floor. Impressive. Now I'm really intrigued." He pressed the fifteenth-floor button and the doors slid shut, trapping us together alone. "Is this a surprise? Or am I allowed to know where we're going?"

"It's a surprise. No security cameras this time, though," I added with a wink.

He groaned and leaned his head back against the elevator wall. "I had no idea about that. Scout's Honor."

"Oh, you're such a jerk, you know that?" Grinning, I grabbed his hand as he did the silly mock salute. Covering it in both of my own, I held it to my brass-covered heart. "Seriously. I want to make this special. No more fights and stupid games. For the next two hours, until we have to meet Lindstrom, there's just me and you."

"And the rest of our lives?" His gaze fell on the ring on my finger. "Does that mean what I think it means? You've made up your mind?" he asked with a twist of his lips, but the pain caused by our separation hovered in the back of his eyes as he looked at me.

"I'm not running anymore," I said, keeping our gazes locked and his hand cupped over my heart.

"I've been scared, and I've been an idiot. But all I've ever wanted is you." I couldn't help the tears that stung my eyes. "I'm so sorry, Lucas."

"Shhh," he whispered as he pulled me close, wrapping me in his arms and his wonderful, warm scent. "I'm sorry too. I should never have pressed you to get married. It's just..." He paused and I could feel the struggle within him through the tension of his muscles as I nestled my cheek against his strong chest. "I love you and I always will. I wanted to have a big celebration. Shout it out to the world. Here's my wife, my family, my heart," he paused. "I wanted my dad to be proud."

Oh, God.

"He'd be very proud of you, Lucas. You're so handsome and talented. Who wouldn't be proud of a son like you?" *Or a husband.* I squeezed him tight in my arms, trembling with the emotion beating through us both. I'd been such a fool, letting my fears cloud my vision to the point I'd lost sight of what truly mattered. Not who was right or who owned whom, but the beautiful love we shared.

The elevator doors slid open as we reached the fifteenth floor. I caught him as we exited, turning him to face me in the soft light reflected by the brass doors.

"I love you with all my heart, Lucas. I want you to know that. But...you aren't expecting me to walk down a church aisle dressed like a meringue, are you?" The idea sent my mind screaming in horror.

"Is it a big wedding that's got you so crazy?" He pulled me into a strong hug. "I can find a different way to spend fifty grand on you and the baby." His chest rumbled as he chuckled, his strong hands stroking my back and snagging on my corset strings. "We'll go to city hall and get a JP to sign the certificate. Make it quiet. If that's what you want."

Except he wanted something memorable, to make his dad proud.

"Ah, hell." I laughed and pulled back a bit so I could look up at his smiling face. So handsome, so sexy, so vulnerable. "I think we're already married anyway. We fight, we laugh, we share the same razor." His brows kinda lowered at that last point, but I pressed on before I lost my nerve. "I know I'm not perfect and I've turned into a jealous shrew just like my mother." I sucked in a deep breath. Feeling a bit dizzy, I jumped off the cliff with both feet. "If it really, *really* means that much to you, then my answer is yes, let's have a big puffball wedding. But, oh my God, Lucas," I added, squeezing my eyes shut tight as panic tightened my belly with visions of my parents' painful divorce. "Don't ever say I didn't warn you. I look hideous in meringue."

"I have to disagree," he said with a sultry chuckle that I felt all the way to my toes. "I'm prepared for the meringue apocalypse. I have a pretty long tongue to rescue you with. And you aren't your mother," he added in a more serious tone, but his lips stayed up at the corners. "You leave your bras hanging in my shower. If she did that it would be just…weird."

"Well, *you* leave your stinky socks on my bedroom floor *and* you snore." I poked my finger in his chest as we wandered down the softly lit hall, hand in hand, looking for room 1501.

"You drool in your sleep," he said, his blue eyes shining bright.

"I do not," I squeaked, embarrassed that he'd noticed.

"Yeah, you do. A little puddle on your pillow right beside your lips. It was there last night when I checked on you."

"You checked on me last night?"

"You left the door unlocked for me," Lucas said. "Why wouldn't I?"

Oh, damn! "But…why didn't you wake me up then?" It would have saved us a heaping bucket full of misery if he had.

"Have you seen yourself in the morning? Grouchy doesn't cut it, prickly-pear." He smiled. "I wanted you to get some sleep. You haven't been well. And I felt bad about how I'd left things on that balcony. I thought we'd have time later to talk...and stuff."

Ah. And then I'd had my jealous freak-out and almost screwed everything up for good. "What kind of 'stuff' did you have in mind?" I asked with a wink.

We stopped outside a door at the end of the hall, the brass plate above the lintel inscribed with *1501: Honeymoon Suite*.

He grinned as he read the sign. "Hot make-up sex?"

"Well, did you know," I said, running my fingers down the shirt covering his belly to play with the fly of his jeans, "that's on my list of *stuff* to do too?"

His scorching gaze raked my body, heating my skin as his grin flashed wide. "Did I mention that's a good look for you? A *really* good look for you?"

Feeling the burn ignite deep inside, my smile broadened into a devilish grin. "Did I mention I'm not wearing any panties?"

All Good Things

WE BARELY MADE it into the room.

Lips locked together, our bodies writhing, Lucas shoved open the door with a bang and half-carried me, half-staggered over the threshold.

My hands were everywhere. Sliding through his hair, pulling at his shirt and exploring the hot, muscular skin beneath. I couldn't get enough of him, his scent, his taste, his tongue in my mouth as it rubbed against mine, the groan he gave as we careened into a wall and broke our kiss, panting.

"Jesus, Casey." He moaned beside my ear, his

big, strong hands slipping over the curves of my body and pulling at the strings cinching my dress. "I want you so bad."

Yeah. I knew exactly what he meant. The urgency to feel his hard, thick cock pounding us both to orgasm clawed at my insides, making my hands shake as I tugged at his pants button.

"Dammit," I hissed as a nail cracked.

He pushed my fingers aside, chuckling. "Let me."

Leaning back against the wall, he released the button on his jeans and undid the zipper, watching my expression as his arousal poked free, tenting his boxers.

"Oh, baby," I said and licked my lips as genuine hunger growled in my belly to taste his smooth length. I slid to my knees, yanking his pants down his hips in the process, and wrapped my hands around his thickness, admiring his heat and strength through his boxers. His fingers caught in my long, wavy curls and I looked up.

"Casey, wait." Eyes dark with passion, chest

heaving, he shook his head. "I won't last. Let me taste you instead." And he tugged on my hair, trying to make me stand up.

To hell with that. I shook my head. No way was I letting this go. After receiving the 'fuckoning' he'd given me yesterday and an erotic massage this morning, I wanted to taste him before claiming more. "You're thinking too much, Lucas," I said with a sassy wink. I slid the tip of my tongue over my full lips. "Just feel."

"Ah hell," he groaned. His nostrils flared. His eyes went wide. His impressive arousal sprang free as his underwear slid down with a quick flick of my wrist. "Look at what you do to me, baby," he whispered.

"Oooh, hello my lovely," I cooed. "Have you missed me?" Raking my nails lightly through the crisp dark hairs on his lower belly, I eased my palms down the taut, veined length of him.

"Fuck," he moaned as his cock jerked beneath my hands.

The tiny slit at the tip glistened. Smiling, I

placed a soft kiss on the biggest vein, enjoying the heat pulsing beneath his skin. Then I slid my tongue to the engorged head of his erection and lapped at the drop of his pre-cum.

He tasted good. Achingly good. His musky, arousing scent filled my mind. "Ah damn." I groaned, licking his tip harder.

Wetness seeped from my core. My thighs trembled, wanting him to be there, thrusting between them. How the hell had I managed without this for three long weeks? Ravenous for more of him, I wrapped my lips around his thick cock, and seized him with my mouth.

He took over then, as I knew he would.

His fingers tangled in my hair, holding me steady while he slipped inside. He loved watching me like this, with the fullness of my mouth wrapped about him, sucking him as he worked himself back and forth between my red, red lips.

Seeing his fierce enjoyment blazing clear in his eyes, the tautness of his neck muscles as his jaw clenched tight, straining for control, to hang on just a bit more while I milked him with my mouth…hell, I couldn't get enough. I squeezed him deep in my throat, moaning with the pleasure of it all. I worked the length of him, licking and sucking. Letting him see how hungry I was. 'Cause I needed to make it up to him, to show him how much I wanted him, prove to him he truly was a super sexy man-beast and that no one would ever love him more than me or make him come as hard.

"Ah, God, Casey." He groaned between clenched teeth. "You're so fucking beautiful."

I held his gaze as I slid one hand from massaging the base of his cock to cup and caress his balls. My fingers danced and played against the sensitive skin near his ass. His eyes misted with passion. His lips parted. I sucked harder, knowing he was close. So quick to come, as he had warned, but so was I.

Reaching down between my legs, I touched my clit.

"Fuck, yes," he said between clenched teeth. His pleasure fueled my pleasure and my pussy creamed as he reared back his head and spurted in my mouth.

I swallowed, moaning, enjoying the hot, salty taste while tremors wracked both of us and he grunted a deep, satisfying groan.

Sweet Jesus, how I had missed this. Tasting his seed, hearing him come, and knowing I had brought him to the brink and beyond. Excitement tightened my core. I wanted to do it all again, and licked his still-hard cock, greedy for every last drop.

"Mmmm, Lucas. I love your cum."

His hands fisted in my long curls, yanking my head up to look him straight in his intense, fiery blue eyes.

"So hungry," he whispered, panting. He licked his lips, steadying his breaths. "What am I going to do with you?"

I flicked my brows sassily as I licked his cock one last time. "Yummy," I moaned. Leaning back on my heels, I fluttered my lashes and thrust my plump, corseted breasts out for him to ogle. "You're the boss. You tell me."

He grinned. "Get on the bed, my gorgeous bunny."

Turning to do as he ordered, I paused. I'd been so intent on tasting Lucas, I hadn't noticed the room. "Oh wow," I whispered, taking in the fairy tale.

It was a canvas of red and cream, accented by gold, flickering candlelight. The bed dominated the room, a heavy four-poster festooned with ivory-colored pillows of various sizes. Sheer gauze panels hung from the ceiling above, draping about the bed like a whimsical dream. Against the wall, a sideboard rested, arrayed with lit tea-light candles—bergamot and vanilla spice, if my nose was correct—a tray of gold foil-wrapped Godiva chocolates, a plate heaped with croissants, two champagne flutes, and an ice bucket with a bottle chilling inside.

"Ginger Ale," Lucas said, with a grin. "Hyacinth thinks of everything. I told you she was good."

"Yes, you did," I agreed with a warm smile. I heard a 'thunk' as he kicked off his boots, followed by the soft whisper of his clothing being removed. But I was too stunned by her thoughtfulness to turn and watch the show.

On the other side of the bed, beneath a wide window, which filled the room with soft afternoon light, a red chaise lounge had been covered with a white faux fur throw and scattered with crimson rose petals. A stack of sketchpads and pencils had been placed on one end. But perched on top, a soft, stuffed, fluffy brown bunny waited, perfect as a baby's first toy.

I covered my mouth with my hand as the room misted.

"Oh, no. No, no, no. Nope," Lucas said. He bent down by my side and scooped me up in his arms as if I weighed nothing. "Come on now, no crying."

"Sh-sh-she bought us a buh-buh-bunny," I sniffled, unable to help myself as he lay me down on the soft covers of the bed.

"Uh-huh." He tossed some of the pillows onto the floor and looked down at me, an easy smile playing across his lips, his fingers stroking my calves. "I'll send her a thank-you note and a hiring contract later. Now roll over. I need to undo that dress."

I wiped my eyes and looked at him, my sniffles vanishing as my pulse spiked. "You're naked," I said stating the obvious. He stood there, brows raised, gorgeous tanned skin glowing in the soft light, with his erect cock standing free and his muscular pecs flexing with laughter.

"Good of you to notice," he chuckled. "Now help me out here before I rip that fucking dress off you."

"Oh my, Mr. Haskell," I giggled, not moving an inch. "Whatever will we do then?"

Growling low, he grabbed me by my stiletto heels and dragged my ass to the edge of the bed. My short skirt pushed up my thighs in the process, revealing the fact I hadn't been joking when I said I wasn't wearing any panties.

He pushed the skirt up more, the pulse in his neck beating fast as he stared at my pale mound peeking smooth and glistening from beneath the crushed black satin. "Ahh," he murmured, swallowing hard. "Now that's beautiful."

Dress forgotten, he dropped to his knees beside the bed and slid his hands beneath my thighs, spreading them wider. Raising my ass, I pulled my dress up more, grinning at his sucked-in breath as he admired the view. God, I loved it when he looked at me like this, his intent gaze dark and hungry, enjoying every inch of my exposed sex. How could I have ever contemplated a life without this? Without him? No one else could *ever* make me feel the way he did right now.

A shiver rippled through me, my stomach clenching with excitement as his fingers danced across my skin, slowly, gently delving inward and exploring my slit. Wetness spread, seeping fresh as my core spasmed in anticipation of him. He smeared my cream over my soft folds, caressing me and teasing me, swirling his thumb close to my engorged, throbbing clit, but not quite touching.

"What would you like me to do now?" he asked.

I pushed my shoulders against the bed, unable to do anything else but arch my back from the pleasure as he blew a breath on my super-sensitive skin.

"Oh God." I moaned, yearning for the mind-numbing release only he could give me. "Lucas, please…"

"Please what?" he teased.

"Fuck me." The sensation flowing from low in my belly spiked as I imagined him hot and hard sliding inside me. *"Please,"* I begged.

"Soon," he whispered, a satisfied chuckle growling in his throat as he massaged my trembling thighs with his hands and teased my slickness with his fingers. I looked down at his face between my legs, at his devastating blue eyes and mussed-up locks of dark hair, and almost came at his hungry, aroused smile. "You smell so good, baby. I need to taste your delicious pussy."

Cupping my ass in his splayed hands, he swept his tongue, warm and gentle along the seam of my folds. But if he meant that to slow things down and sooth my super-heated state, he'd miscalculated how much I needed him now. Spirals of pleasure spread outward from my core as I writhed on the bed, starting a shudder that built with immediate intensity. I fisted his hair in my hands, bucking closer to his face, groaning and demanding more of everything he offered: his tongue licking, touching, kissing, probing, faster, harder, deeper, please, oh God, please, Lucas, *please*—

He wrapped his lips around my clit, teased it with his tongue, and sucked hard.

I screamed, my limbs taut as I arched high.

Sweet Jesus, I thought when I could think again.

He lay naked beside me on the bed, kissing my lips, my jaw, my neck, his hands running over my body, letting me come back to myself, but not completely. A part of me would always be dancing in the sky with him.

"So beautiful," he whispered over and over again like a devotion. "So absolutely beautiful." His hard cock slid against my thigh as he cupped my clockwork-encased breasts and nuzzled my neck, breathing in my scent and tasting my skin. "God, I've missed you, Casey."

Tears whispered silently down my cheeks at the painful yearning in his voice. I'd missed him too, with my body and my soul, and we'd come so close to losing this, to throwing it all away. Never again, never, *ever* again, would I be so blind and stupid.

"I love you, baby," I whispered. "Oh God, I love you so much."

His sexy smile slipped as he looked down into my eyes, his own filled with deep arousal and tinged with uncertainty. "Is it going to be okay? For sex, I mean. With the baby." He placed a little hungry kiss on my lips, making my heart beat fast.

"Oh man," I groaned. Lord save us from noble men and old wives' tales. "Is this why you didn't make love to me after that massage?"

He smiled sheepishly, a lock of his dark hair falling across his forehead and in front of his eyes. "I don't want to hurt you. I wasn't very gentle yesterday."

"I'm not going to shatter, I promise." I brushed his hair aside and grasped his face between my palms, locking his gaze with mine. "And I'll say this as plainly as I can," I added, mimicking his words to me from earlier. "Just so we don't have any more misunderstandings."

His smile spread wide with expectation.

"Sex will not hurt me or the baby. Having no sex for the next nine months will make me a cranky bitch from hell. Understand?"

His eyes blazed. "Yes, my beautiful bride."

"Good," I said and brought his lips to mine for a ravenous kiss. My nausea had gone, hopefully for good, and I had no intention of letting anything get between me and Lucas, ever again.

His mouth was hungry, demanding, answering my urgent need with his own.

I could kiss him like this forever, enjoying his hardness, his taste, his naked heated skin. The way his hands roamed over my body with greedy, seeking fingers. But I ached inside. It wasn't enough. It would never be enough for either of us. Rolling me onto my side, he unknotted my corset and began to loosen the strings.

I sighed with pleasure, feeling everything, *everything* inside my sensitive body, each tug, each rustle, each agonized curse he made as it seemed to take forever to slide apart the ties and undo the clasps at the front. I wanted to beg him to forget the dress, to just slide inside and fill me with his cock. But this was part of the magic he enjoyed, the anticipation, the wait, while he eagerly undressed me.

I lay there letting him, his searing gaze hungry for each new inch of my soft, pale skin.

"Ah, damn," he sighed in appreciation as finally my breasts pulled free from the restricting cups. The dress whispered over my skin and onto the floor. I stretched sinuously, my long hair fanning out beneath me on the bed in a riot of strawberry curls, my body exposed to the cool air and his hot, admiring gaze.

"Jesus, Casey," he said after a moment, his eyes raking every inch of my naked curves. His gorgeous chest heaved as he stared, his toned abs flexing. He rolled over top of me and sat back on his heels between my spread legs. "Your nipples are so thick and dark." Cupping my breast, he bent forward and brought it to his lips.

"Careful," I said, gasping as his tongue rasped over the sensitive tip. "They're a bit sore."

"And goddamn huge. I love it." Lifting my breasts, he brought them together, nuzzling his whiskered face between them. Gently, reverently, he kissed each one. His thumbs rubbed my hard, aching nipples, brushing them over and over, swirling them around.

"Oh," I whispered, biting my bottom lip as intense pleasure and a little bit of pain grabbed low in my belly. I fisted my hands in the covers.

"Too much?" he asked, stopping.

"Mmmm, no, but...I'm not used to how they feel right now."

"I'll fuck them another time, then," he murmured. "But they're just so gorgeous and plump. I could suck them forever." His mouth found my left nipple, surrounding it with his hot wetness. He watched my expression as he gently pulled on it with his lips.

My back arched, pleasure tickling me as he set up a slow sucking rhythm. "Oh God." Not even a hint of pain this time, only desire like I'd never experienced before. A wave of heat flashed over my skin. My fingers snagged in his hair, my breath coming in soft puffs, as he gently suckled me. "That feels so fucking good." I moaned, my head falling backward on the pillow.

He let my nipple go with a little yearning sigh and smeared the wetness he'd left on my breast with his fingers. "I can't wait until they're swollen with milk."

The erotic image hit me so strong, I gasped.

My chest jerked as I pictured him drinking from my full, aching breasts. I'd never thought of that kind of thing as arousing before, but I did now.

He put his hand between my legs, cupping my core. "Baby, you're on fire."

"I think pregnancy makes me horny."

"It makes me horny too." His hard cock twitched against my thigh as if nodding agreement. "You have no idea what it does to me. Knowing you're pregnant with my baby. My beautiful, sexy Casey." Fire danced in his eyes as his gaze swept over my breasts and stopped on my concave belly.

I wrapped my palm around his erection, teasing his veined length. "You filled me with your cum," I murmured, my voice husky as I pictured the sensual sketch he'd drawn of me. "My belly's going to swell for you."

"Fuck," he whispered, jerking a bit as I swept my fingers around his sensitive tip.

"So thick and heavy." I licked my lips, urgency building at his impressive size. "God, I want to taste you again."

A shudder gripped him as my hand slid up and down his shaft, milking him.

His gaze snapped from my belly to stare hot and fierce into my eyes. "Such a naughty, greedy girl." His fingers dipped inside my slit. "Your pussy's dripping wet for me." Licking my cream from his fingers, he smiled.

He spread my folds wide, exposing my heat to the air. "So pretty and pink and tight," he said staring at my exposed center.

My gentle rhythm on his cock faltered as his

fingers touched my nub.

"Your perfect little clit. I love the way it gets hard when you're excited."

Keeping my lips spread wide with one hand, he rubbed his thumb and forefinger along my clit. The hood slid down, exposing the tiny nub beneath to the cool air. I sucked in a sharp breath.

"It's beautiful," he whispered.

My thighs trembled as I struggled to keep from shooting off the bed with the intense sensations coursing through me.

"Do you like this?" he asked. His fingers slipped up and down my nub, stroking me.

"I...I...I..." was all I managed between shuddering breaths.

I couldn't take my eyes off what he was doing with his fingers. Up and down, up and down, slowly and gently. He matched my shaking rhythm on his cock, stroking me as I stroked him, each agonizingly intense pass making me jerk. I couldn't bear it much longer.

"Please, Lucas," I whimpered. My hand

shuddered from his cock. I clutched the bed sheets, my entire body shaking.

"Tell me what you want, love."

"You, just you."

"In here?" His fingers slid from my clit and thrust into my tight channel.

"Yes." My back arched high as I clamped hard around him.

"What about here?" Wiping my slick wetness along the crack of my ass, he danced his finger around my tight sphincter.

"Ooooh, God. Yes. Everywhere," I moaned. He knew all my naughty secrets. "Please just fuck me, Lucas."

"Always and forever," he said.

His mouth pressed against mine, hungry and hot as he positioned himself at the wet opening of my vagina. I wrapped my shaking legs about him as he cupped my ass. I sighed with pleasure, raking my nails down his strong back, reveling in the play of his muscles, and the incredible rightness of his fit with mine.

He paused and lifted his head. I gazed up into his eyes, tears threatening to leak from my own at the look of intense devotion I saw reflected there.

"I love you," we whispered together as we often did at this moment. Then he moved, and with a decadent, moaning, sigh, I welcomed him home.

Bat Guy And Amazon Woman

WE CAME TOGETHER.

We came apart.

We came until the sun had set and a different type of hunger filled us. He fed me croissants and the Godiva chocolates, his tongue licking my sticky lips clean, and then we came again.

Time had no meaning, only the soft whisper of skin on skin and the heat of our beating hearts as we enjoyed each other's moans of ecstasy, reaffirming our commitment over and over and over, until the pain we'd caused each other had faded into a distant bruise and there was only us and our love.

Sated, drowsy, I curled naked on the chaise lounge, my hair a tangled mass of curls, my lips swollen from his kisses, and my limp body draped upon that white fur throw. The light from a nearby lamp cast my supple curves into a shadowy pattern of symmetry, contrasting my pale, sex-flushed skin with the black stilettos on my feet. I yawned, wanting to move, but dared not.

Lucas sat two feet away, butt naked on the plush cream carpet, sketching my post-coitus pleasure. His gaze narrowed in concentration as he studied me, capturing this moment of intense happiness as he saw it through his eyes. Which would be all fine and dandy, except he didn't look happy himself. A frown marred the lines of his gorgeous face.

"Okay," I sighed. "What's the matter? I'm trying not to move." I glanced at his semi-hard cock poking between his crossed legs. "You don't want to go again, do you? 'Cause I think I won't be able to walk for a week. But I might be able to do *something* for you. If you ask nicely." I licked my lips suggestively.

I *was* sore, but from that delicious type of ache caused by well stretched muscles, and there was nothing at all wrong with my mouth. I'd suck him dry, day, evening and night, if he'd let me. So far, my record was six times in one day. But I was certain we could top that.

He shook his head, grinning. "No, my insatiable woman. I'll give you a break. For now." His pencil darted over the sketchpad resting on his thigh. "I just had the feeling I've forgotten something important."

The scent of our lovemaking filled the room, mixing with the bergamot and vanilla spice from the candles. A few of the tea-lights remained lit, burning low, but nothing to be concerned about.

"Did you forget to turn the stove off before you left the loft on Thursday?"

He stopped drawing and threw me a withering look.

"Well, I wouldn't know, would I? I wasn't exactly there." Okay, maybe that hadn't been such a good thing to remind him of, 'cause his look turned into a glare.

He tossed his pencil down and jerked upright, his eyes widening. "Wait a minute. What's the time?"

"How should I know?" I shrugged. "You've still got my phone." Abandoning my pose, I looked around the room but there wasn't a single clock in sight.

"Oh, shit. Goddamn shit, shit. *Fuck*." He yelled. The sketchbook went flying as he jumped to his feet and raced to his pants where he'd left them crumpled in a heap by the wall.

"What is *wrong*?" I cried out, following him, concern making my voice rise.

"*Lindstrom*," he hissed. "I forgot about the fucking deal. He probably thinks I blew him off." Reaching into his pockets, he retrieved his phone and mine. "*Sixteen fucking messages?*" He groaned, closing his eyes. "Oh, that's just fucking great. All this goddamned work for nothing." He tossed my phone at me along with an accusatory snarl. "Next time you decide to seduce me, Casey? *Don't do it on a workday*."

"Don't worry," I snapped back, resisting the urge to rise to that bait. "I won't. Just put your stupid pants on. If we go to him right now, I'm sure we can explain." I looked at my phone.

Astrid had been busy texting me, but thanks to Lucas silencing the tone, I'd never heard it buzzing. It was now just coming up to seven p.m. and she'd sent over thirty messages since about three, all freaking out over the same damn thing. Scrolling through, I started laughing.

"And tell Lindstrom what?" Lucas grabbed his boxers from the floor and slipped them quickly on. "That I lose my mind when you suck me off?" He reached for his socks. "What's so funny?"

"Lindstrom. Oh, my God. You aren't going to believe this... Bat Guy's really Lindstrom," I announced shaking my head, still laughing.

"Well, ho-lee shit," Lucas said, his eyes widening. He dropped his socks on the floor and stared at me. "He's checked us out all weekend completely undercover? Jerk doesn't just think he's Bat Guy. He thinks he's freakin' Wealthy McJackass."

"He slept with my best friend to get the dirt on us," I growled, my laughter dying. I quickly dialed Astrid. It went straight to her voice mail. Shit, *shit!* Was she pissed? Was she dead? I fired off a text for her to call me ASAP.

"Why did you have to silence both our phones?" I accused, pointing my phone at Lucas. "There's this thing that happens called emergencies, you know."

"*Now* do you see why I wanted you to stay away from him?" He pointed a finger back at me. "The guy's a fucking dick."

"I won't deal with him if he hurt her on purpose," I warned, hand on hip, feeling guilty I'd encouraged her to sleep with him. "Even if it means no TV show."

"Don't worry about it. I never liked this from the start. I was only interested in looking at it for business," he muttered. "But if she hasn't kicked his ass, I'll punch the shit out of him myself, deal or no deal. Nobody hurts Astrid. What room's he in?" Ignoring the socks, he grabbed his pants and pulled them on.

I paused, remembering what she'd said about the night she'd spent with the Bat Guy. "Presidential Suite."

"I think that's just down the hall." He headed for the door, naked chest huffing with anger, bare feet padding on the carpet.

"Wait," I cried out. "Goddamn it, Lucas. I'm coming with you." No way was he facing off with Lindstrom alone. Grabbing my dress from the floor, I slipped it on, stuffing my breasts back into the cups, but I needed his help to do it up.

Not wasting any time, Lucas plowed on ahead, ready to race to Astrid's rescue without me, and opened the door.

"Well," she said, standing on the other side, her hand poised to knock. "So, you've come down from the clouds at last." She lowered her hand and raised her brows. With a smile, she waltzed into the room past Lucas.

He gaped in stunned silence.

I had to admit, I understood his gaping. My own jaw dropped at the costume she wore. A classic Amazon Woman eagle-winged red bustier and royal blue star-studded bottoms, complete with tiara, red knee-high boots and golden bracelets at her wrists. *Holy crap.* Astrid had gone rogue and embraced her inner Amazon.

Blue eyes blazing, blond hair brushed over her shoulders, she nodded at me. "Got your text. Thanks for finally returning mine." A giggle escaped her lips as she pulled on the long golden rope she held in her hands, extending out the room. "'Cause this one's got something he wants to tell you." She gave the rope a sharp yank.

I clutched at my dress, holding it up as Race Lindstrom, still in costume, staggered into the room. Coiled in lengths of Astrid's golden Rope of Reality, his arms were trussed to his sides so tight, even the real Bat Guy couldn't escape.

"Go on," she nudged as she tugged him over to her side, his big, powerful frame towering over her tall, thin one. "Tell them."

Lindstrom looked between me and Lucas, his handsome jaw clenched with rage and blue eyes blazing with discomfort. But when they swept over Astrid, his gaze burned with a different kind of heat.

"Go on," she insisted. Pulling the rope tighter, her eyes narrowed to a dangerous slit. "Or I'll leave you like this all weekend and take pictures for your mama."

He licked his lips. "I'm sorry for being a jerk," he muttered, glancing at us again.

"Deceitful jackass," Astrid corrected.

"Deceitful jackass," he snapped, his eyes flashing.

"And..." Astrid prompted, waving her hand for him to continue.

His jaw flexed tighter. "And you can have your TV show. Twenty-four episodes, to start. Retaining creative rights." He looked a bit sick as he said it, but Astrid smiled, blowing him a little grateful kiss.

"Twenty-four?" Lucas asked, surprised. "That's two full seasons."

"Is that syndication?" I whispered. My heart did a little flip. No, not enough for syndication, but we'd be able to make money from royalties from the older episodes. But only if the shows got played. "What about a cancellation clause?" I asked.

Lindstrom shook his head. "That's network, based on numbers. But I'm impressed with the fan base you've already built. You'll both be in on all the decisions of where to take the show. My lawyers will have the contract drawn up this week."

"There now. That wasn't so bad, was it?" Beaming, Astrid patted Lindstrom on the ass and gave it a little pinch. He jumped, his brows lowering, his eyes darkening dangerously as he glared at her. She smiled. "Come on baby," she cooed, her ass wiggling as she sauntered toward the door, pulling Lindstrom behind her on the rope. "It's time for your good-boy reward."

He followed in silence, his attention riveted on her long, slender legs and the way they seemed to go on forever in those *Amazon Woman* boots.

She paused, popping her head back into the room, her hand on the doorknob. "I think I like this cosplaying thing," she said, her cheeks pinkening with a faint blush. "I'll see you guys tomorrow. But I might be a bit late for the convention. All this sex is exhausting." She grinned and blew us a little kiss.

The door clicked shut, leaving us in silence.

"What the hell just happened?" Lucas asked.

"Astrid just bagged us the best deal ever in the history of TV deals," I said.

"Astrid?" he repeated, incredulous. "The blond dominatrix Amazon Woman?"

"Yeah, that's the one," I said. "I think." It was a side of her I'd never before seen but was glad she'd decided to explore.

We both laughed at the craziness of it all, smiling together, happy.

"Well," he said blowing out a breath, his eyes settling on me. "I think we need to celebrate."

I laughed again, letting my dress fall back to the floor as happiness seeped through my skin. "Yeah, we do." I agreed. "An engagement, a baby and a TV deal. Not bad for a day that started out as the worst one of my life."

"Yeah, and it's about to get a whole lot better." Moving to stand in front of me, he cupped my cheeks in his palms and placed a sweet kiss between my brows.

"Really?" I said, swirling my fingers through the hair of his gorgeous chest, tracing his tats.

"Hell, yeah. Come on, I'll help you get dressed up as Steam Bunny."

"Ah," I murmured, thinking of that too-tight bodice. "Is this for me or you?"

"Both," he said as we headed for the dresser where Hyacinth had left our bags. "I promise I'll make it worth your while," he added with a sly smile I felt all the way to my toes.

I caught his hand and pulled him to me, wrapping him in my arms, and inhaling a heavy dose of his intoxicating scent. "I love you, Lucas," I said staring up into his perfect, gorgeous face. "You make me the happiest person alive."

He shook his head. "Impossible. I'm already there, my sexy woman," and he slid his warm hand across my naked stomach to rest over top of the baby. "No one could ever be happier than me with you and our little bunny by my side."

"Make love to me," I whispered, feeling the urgency rise.

"Yes ma'am," he said, his eyes blazing like hot blue fire. "But don't forget the gloves."

"Of course." I grinned. I loved the way he loved peeling off each sensuous layer of my clothes. Leaning up, I kissed his sculpted lips and a little zing of pleasure speared straight to my heart. "The gloves always go on last."

Thank you for reading *Cosplay*, the first book in the Little Miss Kick-Ass series. I hope you enjoyed Casey and Lucas's sexy journey to find their happy ever after.

The following short story, *Super-Sex Me*, continues the series with Casey's BFF, Astrid, in the spotlight. Originally part of the *Secret Hungers* multi-author anthology, (no longer available), I have included it as part of this edition of *Cosplay* for your enjoyment.

What really happened the night Astrid Bitten and Race Lindstrom met?

Read on…

LITTLE MISS KICK-ASS

Super–Sex Me

FELICITY KATES

Astrid

"YOU'D BETTER NOT be peeking," I call out through the cracked-open bathroom door. Cracked-open because my mystery lover has insisted upon listening to the rustling sounds of fabric slipping against my skin while I change into my costume. And mystery lover because we've both decided that keeping his mask on heightens the fun for this evening filled with what I hope will be seriously hot sex.

"Astrid," he says. "You wound me. Why would I ruin the surprise?"

Ah, damn. The man's Scandinavian accent oozes sex, not to mention the ripped muscles, which his superhero costume does nothing to hide. Six-pack abs. I can hardly wait to explore them further with my fingers and tongue. Will his taste be as good as his scent? A woodsy outdoor aroma, which reminds me of a deep forest, and a manly musk that makes my mouth go dry with its deliciousness.

"Oh, you're going to be surprised, all right." I certainly am as I check my reflection in the bathroom mirror. A blond Amazon warrior gazes back at me, wide blue eyes dubious as they take in my ridiculous Amazon Woman costume. A strapless Lycra crop-top with golden bands covers my small breasts. Blue, satin hot pants show off my bare, toned midriff and thighs. A plastic tiara and gold-colored bracelets complete the look.

"Oh, my freakin' God. What the hell am I doing?" I whisper to myself. Playing dress-up with a complete stranger who I met just hours ago? The word 'whim' doesn't quite cut it to describe the leap of faith I've taken. It really isn't my style to be so impulsive, especially with a man I know nothing about and have picked up at a freakin' comic book convention, of all places. I don't even like comic books, or conventions for that matter. The reason I'm at the Fanglorious Fan Expo is to help my BFF, Casey Jackson, get back together with her artist-boyfriend, Lucas Haskell. Not to pick up strange men.

But then Mr. Mysterious arrived, walking toward me through the crowd of convention-goers with his charismatic charm, which has pulled at my insides ever since. No, pull isn't the right word for the intense attraction and mesmerizing effect he's had on me. With my heart racing triple time to keep up, it feels more like an electric shock zinging all the way to my core.

A shock which nearly made me pass out from excitement when he unceremoniously grabbed my ass and asked me to go up to his room for a *fika*.

I slapped him good and hard in return, right on his own tight ass, and exclaimed, "*Jesus*. Did you just ask me to go for a fuck?"

A reaction that seemed only marginally less appropriate when he explained in his sexy accent, "*Fika* is Swedish for a coffee and cake date," and then added with a seriously wicked wink, "But if you'd like a fuck too, I'm more than happy to oblige."

Yeah, wicked. That's a good way to describe him. Wickedly compelling. And right now, I don't mind being compelled into a bit of wickedness.

A semi-hysterical giggle threatens to bubble past my lips.

"Having fun, baby?" he asks through the door.

"You know it, *baby*." I grin, setting the giggle free. "And just how the hell do you know what I'm thinking?"

"It's my superpower. Amongst other things..."

My breath catches at the answering grin in his sexy drawl. "Uh-huh. What other things?" I tease. Well, sort of tease. He's an enigma I have every intention of understanding before the night is through.

"Come out, and I will show you."

What is it about this Mystery Guy that makes me want to do whatever he says and really not care about the consequences? His chiseled features and muscular body? The mesmerizing heat in his sexy voice? The way he kissed me in the elevator ride up to his room? Holy hell, his raw, possessive desire still sizzles though my body, making me anxious for more. Much more.

As Casey pointed out to me earlier, every girl deserves a good time with a seriously hot guy at least once in her life, right? And Mr. Super Suit is unquestionably, seriously hot. Besides, trying something new might be just the thing to get over the string of disappointments my love life has been.

"Are you ready, Astrid?"

"Yes, okay, I'm coming." Smiling at his impatience, I shove my nervousness aside as I open the bathroom door and waltz into the opulent suite.

"Not yet," he murmurs, "but you will be." His voice is a lick of heat as he admires my body, his blue-eyed gaze raking me from head to toe. "You are gorgeous, Astrid."

I laugh and do a little twirl so he can see me from all angles.

He's as gorgeous as I left him before disappearing into the bathroom to get changed. I removed his shirt and pants earlier, under the guise of seeing if the muscles bulging beneath his suit are real. They are. So is the bulge at his crotch, which stands out from the tight black undies he's wearing, supported by lean hips and powerful thighs. His lantern jaw is set in an admiring line, his sculpted lips a wry smile. The black mask hiding the upper portions of his face and head makes his blue eyes shine brighter.

His sun-bronzed skin ripples as he moves toward me, the light brown hairs on his chest heaving as he blows out a low whistle of appreciation. I'm so caught up in watching him, I stumble a little in my three-inch heels.

At five nine, I don't often wear heels as they make me even taller, but he insisted on them to complete the costume. His gaze roams every inch of me, ogling my legs as if he can't get enough of their length. He doesn't appear at all concerned about my height. No giraffe jokes from Mr. Mysterious. What does a six-foot-four guy, built like a UFC fighter, have to feel insecure about? Unless that's a banana shoved in his shorts, every man, woman and geeked-out comic lover at the convention has to be impressed with the size of his package.

He shakes his head, still staring at me. "Your parents couldn't have named you better. You truly are *beautiful as a goddess*. My goddess," he adds and sinks to his knees in front of me on the plush, cream carpet.

"Goddess?" I laugh at his cheesy attempt to impress me with knowing the meaning of my name. "Yeah, but Amazon Woman is a princess, not a goddess. Get your facts straight, geek-boy." He's completely corny and over the top, but the serious way he looks at me makes my pulse race even more.

"Mm-hum," he murmurs. "But you are goddess quality, my Amazon warrior." Capturing my hips in his large hands, he bends his face close to my bare abdomen. "I can't wait to worship you. With my lips..." He presses them against my belly, and I gasp at the warm flush that spreads through my body and fills my breasts, hardening the tips. "And tongue..." he adds. His hot breath puffs against my skin a second before a flick of wetness traces a line downward from my bellybutton to the edge of my satin short-shorts. "And..." As a shiver ripples through me, he stops and looks up at my face, a question in his gaze as it finds mine.

Heart racing, my fingers tighten on his bare shoulders. "And?" I prompt, captivated by the intensity in his dark blue eyes.

"My cock. You want to feel it pulsing inside you, don't you sweetheart?"

I swallow hard, resistance—if I had any in the first place—melting at the passionate and sexy charisma of the man kneeling before me. Shit. He seems to know just what to say, what to do to turn me on. Like a dream lover created for my pleasure. Which can't be true, can it?

Cocking my brow, I gaze at him through

narrowed eyes. "Wait a minute. You aren't some creepy pervert with an Amazon Woman fuck-fetish, are you?"

He presses his forehead against my abdomen, his shoulders shaking with the deep laughter. A teasing smile twists his lips as his gaze finds mine again. "Do you want me to be?"

I shrug lightly, enjoying the easy openness of being with him. "Maybe." He does make a mighty fine Bat Guy. But right now, I'm more interested in finding out what secrets are hidden beneath his mask.

As if sensing my mood, he grabs my hand and presses my palm to his lips. "You are a treasure, Astrid. Come on," he prompts. "Your treat is ready."

He rises in one fluid movement and draws me by our joined hands to the small dining nook nestled in a corner of the Chicago Marriott's Presidential Suite.

Sheer drapes veil the windows, shrouding the jewel-like city view. Open French doors lead into the king-sized bedroom, with its extravagant four-poster and Egyptian linens. The entire suite screams money. Clearly, Mr. Mysterious has expensive tastes and a bankroll to fulfill them.

He's said he's in business, but what business he has yet to reveal.

I follow him, breathless and slightly dazed by the sudden track my life has taken and the man who's offered me the ride.

Thus far, the *fika* has consisted of a truly breathtaking make-out session on his couch and a delicious dinner brought by room service. Herbed chicken with cashews, mushroom-infused quinoa and a crisp bottle of excellent white wine.

"Dessert," he promised at the time as he watched me eat the last morsel of dinner on my plate. "Will be something special."

I like the idea of a secret treat, but I can't imagine what could possibly top the experience of getting dressed up as superheroes for a date. I didn't come to the convention prepared to be part of the cosplayer crowd, but it's oddly exciting to be dressed so outrageously. Then again, I'm more than ready for a bit of excitement in my life, odd or otherwise.

"This looks yummy," I say as my gaze roams the linen-draped table. The empty dinner dishes have been cleared away. It's now covered with a fresh bottle of wine nestled beside two ornately decorated silver bowls, chilling on ice.

"Elderflower cream and Swedish strawberries." His voice holds a distinct note of pride about conjuring up what is obviously to him a delight.

"Elderflower?"

His exultant expression dims as his gaze finds my blank stare. "You've never tried it before?"

I snort as I take the seat he offers me. "I'm about as Swedish as an Ikea meatball."

His head cocks to the side as he studies me with that penetrating gaze of his, the one which seems to look into my soul. "Interesting. You seem very...northern."

"My grandparents are from Sweden. But I was born in New Hampshire."

"On a dark and stormy night?" He grins as he takes his own seat.

I shake my head. "Nope. The stork dropped me off in May. That's an interesting tattoo," I say, turning the conversation to more relevant things. "Is that a deer antler?"

He glances down at his left shoulder, where a dark, branching pattern stains his golden-tanned skin. "Reindeer. And it's a birthmark." He uncorks the bottle of wine and refreshes our glasses.

"Birthmark? Really? That's different. Good thing it's not a 666." I snicker, thinking of Damien's mark from the horror movie *The Omen*, which is the only one I've ever heard of being a recognizable pattern, and it didn't herald good things.

"Yes," he murmurs. His fingers brush mine as he passes across my glass, stirring a tremor of fire at the touch. "Tell me more about your friends."

I blink. Dinner was filled with similar chit-chat. Back and forth questions and friendly banter. He seems endlessly curious about my life, as if genuinely interested in getting to know me before going any further. Personally, I'd rather have been slammed against the wall and had wild monkey sex as soon as we reached the room, but it appears he needs a bit more time to get comfortable. Who'd have guessed that Mr. Sexy Scandinavian Bat Guy would actually be a bit of a gentleman?

I roll the cool stem of the glass between my fingers. "Okay...my friends. Well, Lucas is a really talented artist and Casey is his promotional assistant. I've known her for years. She's very beautiful. Models for him and stuff, you know? I'm helping them sell their books."

He takes a sip of wine, looking at me over the rim of his glass. "Do you like it?"

"Helping them? Yeah, they're good people. I'm not really interested in comics, but from what I can see, *Steam Bunny* does okay." I lean forward in my chair, happy to share the exciting news for my friends. "Actually, Lucas is meeting some bigwig from L.A. at the convention this weekend, to sign a TV animation deal."

He smiles. "Wow. That's exciting."

"Yeah, I don't know if it will go through though."

"Why not?"

"Well, I've never met him myself, but Casey says the L.A. guy is rumored to be a bit of a prick."

He sets his glass onto the table, his eyes studying me, and I swear his brows flick beneath his mask. "A prick?"

I nod. "You know how it is with big business types. Only in it for the money. A different girlfriend every night." As I lower my voice to a conspiratorial whisper, I can't resist leaning even closer toward him and his intoxicating scent. "To be honest, it sounds like he has control issues and is seriously scared of commitment."

His eyes flash with deep heat. "That's a very interesting theory. And what are you scared of?"

The earnest way he asks the question makes my skin prickle, as if my answer is very important to him. Caught off guard, I blurt out the truth. "Getting my heart broken. Again."

"Ah." He sits back in his seat, a knowing twist to his lips. "I'm sorry. Sounds like you've dated the wrong men."

"Always." As the pain of my many disappointments and betrayals twangs my heart, I grip the stem of the glass harder and look at the berries instead of him.

"Not always," he corrects. "Not this time."

His thoughtful tone draws my gaze to his again. As he strokes his fingers along the line of his steely jaw, I can't help wishing they are stroking me instead.

"Do you trust me, Astrid?"

"Um, no." An awkward laugh bubbles out of my throat. "We've only just met."

"Have we? It feels like much longer. I think we need to test this attraction."

"Test?"

"Explore. Indulge...enjoy."

"Enjoy..." The word swirls around my mind as I savor it with the same decadent interest with which it's been said. "I could go for that." I raise my glass of wine. "To good sex," I announce.

"To *great* sex," he corrects, and his glass meets mine with a delicate *clink*. Eyes locked on his, I take a sip at the same time he does. The crisp liquid slides cool and easy down my throat, causing a warm buzz to flow through my body. Or maybe that's from the dizzying intensity of him.

He licks his lips and sets his glass on the table. "I want to show you so many things. Give you so much pleasure. But I need you to trust me a little. Do you think you can?"

"I'm...not sure. What do you have in mind?"

"I want you to sit on your hands," he says quietly.

"What?" I set my glass down before it spills.

He rises from the table and moves to stand beside me. "Sit on your hands," he repeats, "and whatever happens, don't move them until I say."

I look up his imposing wall of sexy muscle to his face. "Ah...that's a bit, um, He-man-ish, isn't it?"

"Well, I could tie them with your Rope of Reality." He indicates the thin gold-colored rope, which came as part of my costume, coiled at my hip. "But I think you'd prefer not, am I correct?"

"Um, yes."

"The important thing is for you to resist the temptation to touch anything until I say so. Okay?"

"I—okay. Sure, I guess." But already I'm obeying, my pulse thudding with anticipation as I slide my fingers beneath my satin-covered butt cheeks and pin my hands to the seat.

He smiles. "Now. I want you to close your eyes."

"W-Why?"

"Seeing isn't always believing. When you don't have your eyes to fool you, everything else becomes sharper. Clearer. Touch, taste, scent. Your body becomes more sensitive." He nods at the bowl of strawberries waiting patiently on the table. "These are going to be the most delicious berries you've ever tasted."

I pause as excitement mixes with doubt. "I take it you've done this kind of thing before?"

"Not like this. Not with you." His deep blue eyes search my face. "This will probably work best if I blindfold you."

Oh shit. I swallow hard and follow his movements with avid interest as he picks up one of the large, white linen napkins from the table. "Um, I'm not into any kinky BDSM stuff. Just so you know."

"Have you ever had an orgasm so intense you thought you'd pass out?"

"No," I whisper, my face heating at his knowing gaze.

He grins. "That's what I'm into. Just so you know."

Holy hell. My mouth goes dry, making it necessary to lick my lips before I can speak. "You are a very naughty man, you know that?"

Being around him feels a bit like I'm being sucked into a dizzying vortex, one that I don't mind being consumed by.

Laughter rumbles through his muscular chest, making his taut pecs flex, but his expression quickly grows serious once again. "Will you permit me to give you pleasure, Astrid?"

"I can take the blindfold off whenever I want to?"

"Of course. The choice will always be yours."

The world narrows as time slows and moves with my pulsing heartbeats. His dark, bottomless pupils are mesmerizing, flickering with a hungry fire I crave to know. Everything hinges on this moment. My choice, my answer, my future. It's just sex, yet not. I know it in my soul, the craving, the calling. For him. This stranger, yet not stranger. This man built like a Viking sex god incarnate. Can I trust him? The unknown beckons, illicit and powerful. Fear shivers down my spine, but that fear isn't for him.

I give him the only answer I can. "Yes."

"Thank you."

The brush of his lips atop my head sends a pulse of heat down my spine. Flexing my hands beneath my butt cheeks, I suck in a deep breath as he bends on one knee beside me. At the soft caress of his fingers against my hair, I struggle not to tremble from the anticipation that ripples through me. Then he places the napkin over my eyes, committing me to darkness.

"Is it too tight?" His voice is whisper-soft, tickling my ear with velvet heat as he fastens the knot, and this time I can't resist a pleasure-filled shiver. God help me, but I swear if this man's voice gets any sexier, I'll die happy from a thousand orgasms.

I shake my head, testing the strength of my bonds. The blindfold doesn't shift, but it also doesn't pinch. "No. It's fine."

"Tell me how you feel."

"Nervous. Excited." My heart pounds so loud in my ears, I'm sure he must be able to hear it. I can move my hands if I want to, anytime I want to, and uncover my eyes. The choice to remain in the dark is empowering, the act of trusting this man, even more unexpectedly so. "I feel..." I swallow hard. "I feel alive."

No, more than alive. It's like my whole world is expanding with new vision. His delicious heat surrounds me, fills my mind as I inhale a heavy dose of his arousing scent. Can he smell how hot I am for him?

My nipples are achingly hard and tight, my bare skin flushed with goose bumps, and I'm wet, wetter than I've ever been between my legs as I wait in the darkness for him to speak, move, do something to ease the need building inside me.

I want to come at the hands of this man.

This very exceptional man.

He shifts ever-so-slightly, one hot palm resting easy on the nape of my neck. His other hand does something with the bowl of berries.

I strain, my whole body listening as something sweeps through the cream with a wet flourish. The combined scents of his wild, alpine earthiness and the berries assault me, and I lick my lips, ravenous to taste all he has to offer.

"Hungry, my goddess?"

"For you? Yes."

His fingers caress the sensitive hairline at the nape of my neck, and I barely stifle a moan as the gentle touch moves through every inch of my body.

"Good," he murmurs, his sexy voice full of delicious intent. "Now, I want you to open your mouth."

AS I GIVE the ripe berry a second pass through the thick, lustrous cream, I study Astrid Bitten's beautiful, upturned face and plump, red lips, and silently curse my good luck.

Of all the places and all the times to find *her*, why the hell did it have to be now?

My business at the convention is just that—business, not pleasure. But the erotic pull was so strong my cock hardened as soon as I walked inside the hotel convention hall.

At first, I thought it was for her beautiful friend Casey, whom I came all the way from L.A. to meet. But one glimpse of Astrid, and I recognized the truth. Here she is, the answer to my prayers at long last. My match, my true mate...and she has no clue who I am. Not even a glimmer. Probably because she's as clueless as clueless can be about herself.

So now I have the challenging task of enlightening her without making her run screaming for the hills, or the nearest bodily weapon. She is, after all, a goddess in spirit. Her lithe, fit figure practically oozes unearthly sensuality. But experience has shown me that people generally don't want to know they have a bit of supernatural born inside them, and when faced with the truth, they often react...badly.

Maybe that's part of my penance? I've never known the gods to be overly interested in fairness. Not that I've ever personally known a god. But the influence their confounding will has on my life? Yeah, that's something I'm very familiar with.

I smile, empowered by pleasure as Astrid's

supple, parted lips tremble while she blindly waits to see what I'll place inside her generous mouth. A thousand erotic ideas consume me, and I have to fight to stay focused on the need to go slow. She's so damned responsive and trusting, it blows my mind. But I must tread very carefully here. Very, very carefully. Not force or sway her choices.

No matter how much the need to use my inherent supernatural abilities screams through my blood, I have to bite down on the burning desire to unleash my special influence and bind her to my will.

As talents go, the ability to impose my desires on the world around me has made me billions in business, but in matters of love it's been a disaster. My selfish, immature need to create the perfect mate destroyed my wife. I'd rather face an eternity in hell than make that mistake ever again. Even if it would make things easier once Astrid discovers that I am, without a doubt, the big-wig prick from L.A. whom she unwittingly described.

Control? Yes, I'll admit I'm addicted to having that over things, especially in the bedroom, but commitment issues? I have no problem committing to Astrid. She's my destiny, and the connection between us glows like an ember of hope in my soul that I'd be a fool to resist.

The revolving door of women who've gratified my body since my wife's death have been nothing more than a moment's absolution from the loneliness which consumes me. I would much rather be consumed by Astrid.

Admittedly, I should probably be upfront with her, tell her who I am, and what business has brought me to the convention. But why hurry the inevitable storm? Especially when I can give her so much pleasure before then.

So. Much. Pleasure.

Her nervous breaths puff against my fingers as I bring the cream-drenched berry to her lips. Her pink tongue flicks out to taste my offering, and she tenses as she decides what the flavor is, and if she likes it.

My already hard cock becomes even harder at the thought of that little pink tongue tasting me. I'm consumed by the image of her tiny pearl teeth gently grazing my tip as she takes me inside her mouth like the strawberry. The idea imprints itself on my mind so strongly, I grind my teeth together to stifle the groan filling my soul.

"Mmmmm," she murmurs as she wraps her lips around the ripe fruit and sucks the cream off it.

"You like it?"

She nods and takes the whole strawberry in her mouth, and I watch, mesmerized by the slender line of her throat as she chews and swallows.

"More," she demands and licks cream and juice from her lips with a seductive sweep of her tongue.

Goddamn. Okay, well maybe I used a bit of energy and influenced things by encouraging the berries to be the sweetest, most succulent fruit they can be and the whipped cream the richest and smoothest possible. But it's all for the good of giving her the most pleasurable evening of her life.

That has to count as being okay, doesn't it?

It's not like there's any other way to get fresh, sun-ripened Swedish strawberries in early March at a moment's notice.

"This is really delicious," she murmurs, and a faint flush brightens her pale cheeks. "I've never tasted anything like it before."

I scoop up a dollop of the soft whipped delight with my finger and touch it to her bottom lip. Her mouth closes, trapping my finger inside. The tip of her tongue lazily plays around my digit as she sucks me clean before releasing me with a wet *pop* and sultry grin.

A pulse of heat flares in my groin and spreads through my entire body. Snatching up the bowl, I hold it to her lips.

"Eat," I command.

Her tongue dutifully flicks out, probing and licking the white decadence I offer. I move the bowl away, making her reach with her tongue and mouth to lap up the cream like a hungry kitten. She follows it down onto the table.

"That's it, baby, show me how you like to use that saucy tongue of yours."

Her tiara and blindfold hold her long, golden hair

away from her face, giving me a good view of her sexy licks and moans as she lazily explores the cream.

Fuck, she's glorious. Her hands dutifully pinned beneath her bottom. The blindfold covering her eyes. She quivers with the strain to hold steady while she indulges my whim and feeds her own. I don't give two shits about what costume she's wearing. In fact, I'm dying to see what secrets are hidden beneath it.

I slide my hand along her spine and hook a finger beneath the edge of her Spandex top. Then I give it a sharp, downward yank.

Release. I silently command the fabric using all the authority I was born with when I came screaming into the world on a stormy winter's night. A harsh gasp shudders through Astrid as her top immediately obeys and falls onto her lap in pieces.

She arches back in her chair, her shoulders giving a sharp jerk as she fights the urge to move her hands from beneath her ass and cover her exposed breasts instead. Her mouth opens, but no words escape.

"Hush, baby," I whisper. "You are beautiful."

She shakes her head, anxiety making her tense. "I'm—they're too small."

"No," I reassure her, dropping to my knees at her side, my gaze fixed on her creamy, unblemished skin and pale pink nipples. I coax her to turn her body sideways and face me. "You are perfect," I insist, "gorgeous."

Palm-sized breasts, and I have big hands to measure by. The ideal fit for her tall, thin frame. She's strong and lithe, with flawless skin, and I clench my jaw against the desire burning hot to ravish her. The need to make her mine has sizzled through my veins since the moment I spied her sitting all prim and proper and completely out of place in the hotel convention hall.

I could end the game now and just fuck her 'til she screams in pleasure. Yank those Amazon Woman bottoms down and thrust my hard cock inside her heat. It's what we both want. But then I'll lose this chance of getting to know her and seeing what things give her greatest pleasure. A rare treat like Astrid Bitten is meant to be savored, not rushed.

Goose bumps ripple across her body as I lazily trace my fingers along her collarbone, reveling in the softness of her skin and the sweeping upward curve of her breasts. Her nipples tighten, hard buds becoming even harder.

"Tight little alpine berries," I murmur appreciatively. "I wonder if they taste as sweet?"

A flick of my tongue against her skin is rewarded with a rich, moaning gasp from deep within her body. Holding her steady with my palm on her supple back, I give the same attention to her other nipple, enjoying her moans as I graze the hard tip with my teeth.

"Shit," she whispers, her hands flexing beneath her sweet ass. "What are you doing to me?" She presses her thighs together.

I thrust them apart and move closer, positioning myself between them, and filling my mind with her warm, honey-sweet scent.

"Do you want me to stop?" I ask, enjoying the flush of heat that stains her skin as I blow a breath against her wet, erect nipples.

"Hell, no." Her voice is throaty with the desire radiating from her in waves. She wants me, hungers for the release I can give her. On impulse, I crush a strawberry between my thumb and fingers and smear the pulp on her pink nipples, painting them bright red—a stark arousing contrast to her pale skin.

"Oh, sweet baby Jesus," she whispers, her strong thighs pressing into my sides as she shifts and squirms. "Those berries are freakin' cold."

"Ah...you prefer heat?"

I envelope one pert nipple with my mouth and suck hard, allowing the hungry fire burning through my veins to flare into her. I'm rewarded with a sharp cry and a tremor of pleasure that moves through her body and back into mine, continuing the circuit of erotic energy connecting us.

The combination of sweet juice and her fragrant

skin intoxicates me, but her decadent moans are my undoing as I feast, sucking and licking her clean. I can't help the urgency of my movements as I grasp her tighter with my mouth and hands, seeking every bit of pleasure her sounds of enjoyment give me.

Shit, I'm hard. My balls full and heavy. Powerful. The desire to fill her with my seed throbs in my groin. I'm going to make her drip when she comes. Going to make her scream.

I focus my need as a thought, and my underpants instantly obey, falling to the carpet in shreds. It doesn't matter. I can always buy more, and the brief expenditure of energy is quickly replenished by Astrid's uninhibited pleasure. Grasping my thick cock, I slide my palm up and down the taut length, and groan.

Feeling her stiffen slightly, I pause in my exploration of her breasts to look at her flushed face.

Her lips part in blatant interest. "Are you—?"

"Stroking myself? Yes. You're a very beautiful woman, Astrid."

"Oh, my God! I knew it. You do have some kinky Amazon Woman fuck-fetish, don't you?" She bounces up and down on her hands in excited laughter, causing her breasts to jiggle, and another wave of fierce desire grips me.

"Kinky?" I rasp. "Yes. I guess you could say I enjoy certain pleasures." And I catch her nipple in my mouth and gave it a tender nip, causing her squirms to still. "But I asked you to dress up in the costume..." Moving close to her ear, I let my voice drop to a whisper. "Because I wanted to see if you would do it. Personally, I think you look sexiest with your clothes off."

I stroke my length up and down again, my cock growing even thicker as she listens intently. Her expression changes from enraptured to almost painfully aroused as the sound of skin rubbing on skin electrifies the air between us.

The pulse at her throat beats erratically, and I imagine her pupils are wide and unfocused with desperate need as they stare blindly into the darkness beneath the blindfold. The image makes me grip my cock tighter, and a deep moan rumbles through me.

"Use the cream," she chokes out.

Oh, baby! I already know she likes to give orders, but the husky way she says that command fans my blood into an inferno of fiery need. Standing, I sweep a generous dollop of the elderflower cream onto my palm and smooth it over my erection.

Cold and wet, the cream slides between my fingers as I work it up and down my taut skin and try not to pass out from the intense sensation. Fucking hell, I've never been this aroused before, but watching her get so turned on by the sound of me jerking off is fast becoming an addiction.

Her lips part slightly as the slippery cream responds to my touch, moving and sliding sticky wetness over my cock. Fragrant elderflower and her potent honey-sweet arousal scent the air, but what entrances me the most is the look of absolute hunger on her face as she follows the sound of my movements.

"How does it feel?" she whispers.

"Fucking incredible," I choke out, my voice sounding haggard and needy to my own ears. "You have no idea what you do to me, baby." Have I ever experienced a more erotic moment in my life? Of course not. I've never been with Astrid Bitten before today, and she owns my soul.

"Oh, God." Her tongue darts out to lick her lips. "You smell so good. I want to taste it. I want to taste you." She squirms in her seat, her desperation to be free of the promise that pins her hands to the chair escalating with each panting breath. Her nostrils flare as she opens her mouth and leans toward my groin, seeking my cock.

Holy fucking shit. I stand, transfixed, as my tip brushes her cheek, leaving behind a streak of whipped cream. My hot breath bursts from my lungs while she blindly fumbles, her mouth chasing my cock as it bounces and jerks. At the exquisite torture, stars explode behind my eyes. I grab my cock to steady it as her mouth finds its mark.

"Finally," she says and gives my erection a long,

appreciative lick.

"Ah, baby." I twine my trembling fingers in her silky, golden hair as she licks the cream off me in slow, agonizingly blissful strokes. My breath catches in my lungs, becoming uneven gasps.

"God, you're fucking huge," she says, her voice raspy with desire. "I love it," she adds with a cheeky smile and wraps her lips around my thick tip, probing the tiny slit with her tongue.

"Fuck it," I hiss through clenched teeth as my balls clench. There's was no way I can last if she takes me all the way in her mouth, no way I can resist her plump lips and the magical way she works her tongue.

Scooping her up in my arms, I have her out of the chair and planted against the wall in two quick strides.

Her hands snake around my back and roam upward, her fingers grasping the edges of hair sneaking from beneath my Bat Guy mask. She nibbles my neck hungrily as her long legs wrap around my waist. Her stiletto boots hook over my ass, and she pulls into a snug fit against my throbbing groin, as if she's always been meant to be there.

A groan fills me at the blissful feeling of her damp satin bottoms pressed against my cock. God, those legs. They go on for miles. Curvy and slender yet gorgeously strong. So much for the idea of going slow and exploring all her pleasure zones. I can't bear another second without my dick buried deep inside her.

"I take it I can touch you now?" she asks breathlessly.

"Hell, yeah." She doesn't need to ask permission. She's always been in total control.

Her lips dance hungrily along my jaw as her fingers press against my skin. "That was fun," she murmurs beside my ear in a hot whisper, "but I like using my hands better."

She caresses my back, my arms, my neck, running her nails though the short hairs on my nape as if she can't get enough of touching me.

And I must admit the feeling is mutual as I hold

her in place against the wall, my hips slowly pressing my straining cock against her hot, deliciously fragrant pussy.

I need those Amazon Woman shorts off. Now.

Moving my cock away from her groin, I look down at the blue, satin fabric, and concentrate. It disintegrates into shreds at a thought, the fibers instantly obeying my mental command to separate. But those fuck-me heeled boots crossed over my back? Yeah, they can stay. She has the most gorgeous legs I've ever had the pleasure of being entrapped by.

She tenses at the sudden lack of clothing. "What the—?" she squeaks, glancing downward as if she can see through the blindfold.

"I'll buy you new ones," I say.

"But how did you—?"

"Does it matter? 'Cause now I can touch you, baby."

I grasp her gloriously naked ass in my hands and push against her gorgeous pussy. My length rubs along her slit and she stills, her mouth opening in a delicious moue of bliss-filled surprise. Her expression intensifies with a sweet agony that echoes my own as I set up an undulating rhythm with my hips. Back and forth, I gently rub her wetness, my shaft sawing deliciously over her clit.

An unintelligible whimper passes between her plump, parted lips.

"I know just how you feel, baby."

Goddamn it. She feels so good with her moist heat cradling me that I'm consumed with how it will feel to be inside her. I need to fill her with my seed and leave my mark, branding her as mine. But I need to protect her more. I sense that she's clean and healthy, disease is not an issue. Condoms won't help with that anyway. My sperm just blasts right through them. But I can't take the chance of a pregnancy.

Not now.

Not until she knows the truth about my past and makes the choice.

Maybe not even then.

I lick stray cream off her cheek and nuzzle her

ear. "You're using protection pills, Astrid?" It's more of a statement than a question as I sense the answer already. But I need verbal confirmation, to know she firmly believes she's protected by their power. If not, I'll have to forgo enjoying her sweet pussy for the tightness of her ass. Pills aren't perfect as a barrier against my seed, but if she believes in them, I can control the rest. For now.

She pulls out of the erotic daze she's in, a slight frown touching her lips. "Quarterly shots. I don't trust pills. Especially not after what's happened to Casey."

"Casey?" I murmur absentmindedly, my concentration fully captured by the woman in my arms. I nibble on her earlobe and keep up my slow rhythmic friction against her slit.

She gasps slightly, her words coming in a breathless rush as she says, "She's pregnant. She doesn't think so, but she is. I can tell."

A jolt of surprise ripples through me, making my cock throb as I pull back to look at her flushed cheeks and serious expression. "You can tell?"

She nods. "I dunno how. I just always can. Even before I—" She stops, her frown deepening for a second before she shrugs it away. "Well, it doesn't matter. You don't need to worry. I can't get pregnant."

Can't or won't? The question ricochets in my mind even as the answer chases after it. My entire being relaxes at the same time as the desire to claim her roars full throttle through my veins. Of course, the gods always have enjoyed a sense of humor. But here, now, in this beautiful woman wrapped tight around me with her gorgeous sexy soul, they have given me a second chance.

The hope flaring in my soul lodges dangerously in my heart.

Childbirth. Fertility. She can control them, and if I were a betting man—which I am—I'd bet she bears the mark somewhere on her body. A symbol which confirms her lineage in the same way my reindeer birthmark speaks volumes about mine. I haven't found hers yet, but a smile tips my lips at the thought of how much fun I'm going to have, exploring every inch of her silky skin, looking for it.

"*Sarahkka*," I breathe against her full, kiss-hungry lips as my whole world suddenly makes perfect sense.

But my golden-haired goddess digs her nails into my shoulders with a fierce, painful grip.

Astrid

"WHO THE HELL is Sarah?" I bellow, practically deafening my own ears. What kind of a dumbass calls out the name of one girl while having sex with another? I can handle many things, but not that. I press my nails deeper into his skin, drawing blood and not caring if he feels pain. Stupid dumbass deserves it and more.

The agonizing rhythm of his cock pressing and rubbing my clit falters but becomes strong again as he regroups with a smile in his voice. "Not, Sarah.

Sarahkka. In ancient Sami culture, she's a respected goddess of childbirth. You remind me of her."

"Oh..." Well, shit. My anger leaves in a whooshing breath, but frustration remains. Can he not get over this goddess crap and just get down to the business of fucking me? "I want this blindfold off. Now," I demand, retracting my nails from his skin.

"Yes," he agrees, not missing a beat. "I want to see your eyes when you come."

I blink against the sudden brightness when, as if by its own accord, the blindfold falls from my eyes and the world becomes visible. My heart skips a beat as I catch his avid stare.

"Let's move to the bedroom," he says.

As he braces his arms beneath my ass and starts to move away from the wall, I press my nails into his shoulders again.

"No. I want it here," I blurt in a rush. At his astonished look, I feel my cheeks heat. "Please?" I add as guilt about the red crescents my nails have made on his sun-bronzed skin flushes through me.

Bending forward, I lick one of the marks I made, tasting the tang of blood, and feeling a tingle deep in my belly as he sucks in a sharp breath.

So silly after all the things we've already done with the strawberries and cream, not to mention the impromptu blindfold, but being held like this by him is more than just exciting. I've never had sex against a wall before. It doesn't usually work well with my giraffe-length legs, and most guys can't hold me up long enough. But Mr. Oh-my-goddess Sexy Man hasn't even broken out in a sweat.

"The choice will always be yours," *...my goddess.* The unspoken title whispers in my mind, clear in the adoring and sultry look in his eyes.

I want to beg him to stop calling me that. I'm not a goddess any more than I'm really Amazon Woman or able to fit into size six shoes. It's a physical impossibility. Gods and goddesses belong in myth and folklore. They don't really exist, and I thought at first that he was making it up as a kind of sexy joke. But what if he really believes it?

The question is tossed from my mind as he traps

me against the wall again, his big body and mouth covering mine with his seemingly indomitable strength.

Something shifted while I was tied up, giving me an awareness I've never experienced before. Has the forced lack of control over my eyes and hands made me feel so alive, or is it the man I'm with, thrusting his large cock against my greedy pussy that makes me crave everything he can give me and more?

I know him.

Know him, in my soul and I can't shake the somewhat frightening feeling that there is a whole lot more going on here than casual sex.

Hell, does it matter?

All I truly crave right now is the way his fierce, hungry lips mold mine, and having him embedded inside me.

Really freakin' soon.

Never in my life have I felt this excited or been so wet. I'm certain he must smell my dripping need. He seems to have a sixth sense about everything concerning me. And I have no doubt that he enjoys every bit of my pleasure with the way he swallows my whimpers and coaxes out more by nibbling on my bottom lip.

He holds me anchored against the wall, my hips supported by his strength. One strong hand clasps my ass while the other holds my head in place.

I can't get enough of the feel of his smooth, tight skin and the way it plays over his hard muscles when he moves. Releasing my lips, he sucks in a ragged breath and glances down at the junction of our bodies.

"I love this." His voice is thick with desire as he tugs on the little tuft of blond hair that nestles above my clitoris. "It's so sexy. It makes me want to fuck you even more."

His thumb swirls through the wisps of hair, making my thighs tremble with the intimate caress so near to my swollen nub, not quite touching, but massaging the skin around.

God, it feels divine.

He feels divine.

So strong and hard and perfect. If he would just move his thumb a bit lower I would probably—

"Look at me, Astrid." The command in his voice leaves no choice in the matter, and glancing up, I find his soul-shattering stare trained on me. Wide, shadowy pupils gaze back at me, threatening to swallow me with the fire that I want so desperately to be consumed by. "I'm going to take you now, baby. I'm going to make you mine. Okay?"

Okay? I nod dumbly. How the hell would it not be okay, but he seems to need me to say it. "Yes. Please. Fuck me now." My body throbs so badly for him, I ache. And I don't even know his name. Or anything else about him. But fuck it; I've lost the will to care.

Without breaking eye contact, he catches my wrists in one of his strong hands and lifts them above my head. Then, angling his groin, he brings his erect cock to the wet entrance of my sex.

Shifting my hips to give him better access, I wrap my legs about him tighter. The thick, veined length I explored with my tongue nudges inside my tight opening. I gasp at the sensation that shoots through me as my skin stretches to accommodate his welcome intrusion. Nine months of only a vibrator are no comparison to this.

With a deep, feral growl, he thrusts inside and buries himself to his root.

"Ahhh," I gasp as I arch backward, my head pressing against the wall, at once weak and powerful from the fullness of him. Having his cock inside me feels agonizingly good. Like a white-hot poker of blissful sensation that only grows better when he withdraws slightly then pushes inside me again.

"Astrid," he hisses.

"You feel so amazing." I moan the truth as tears blur my vision. "Oh baby, please."

His answer is something which sounds vaguely Swedish mixed with an unintelligible, guttural groan. His face tenses, then becomes suffused with fierce arousal as he sets up a slow rhythm, giving me time to adjust to his size.

I need to come so badly, but with my arms

pinned above my head, I can't reach down and help things on their way. Then again, with the way he moves his body with mine, I don't need to. His cock rubs all my sweet spots as he gently increases his pace, each powerful stroke stoking the fire that engulfs us.

I've never come during sex before, not without someone rubbing my clit. Never felt so full and complete. But I can't contain the excitement and heat building inside much longer, and I know I'm on the threshold of something powerful.

"My goddess," he moans with hoarse need. "My Astrid. So tight and perfect. I could fuck your pussy forever." Sweat dampening his skin, he tugs on my nipple between his teeth.

I cry out as he licks my hard peak, swirling his tongue round and round the tip.

Pinned to the wall by his hand on my wrists, his mouth on my breast, and his cock inside me, I have no choice but to give myself over to him, and no desire not to.

He pounds me hard and fast as he ravages my

flesh with his lips, his steely muscles holding me in place.

My eyes drift shut as the pressure builds, spreading outward in waves of pulsing heat from my core. I struggle to catch my breath as moan after mewling moan escape my parched throat with each hard thrust. His groans of pleasure mix with mine, heightening my arousal with the knowledge he's right there with me and consumed by the same urgent need.

"Sweetheart," he murmurs in his enchanting voice, and the sexy sound makes my control begin to fray. His mouth moves up from my breast and finds the pulse at my neck. He licks the erratically beating vein. "Let go for me, baby. It's time to let go."

His teeth lightly graze my skin as he sucks hard against my neck and buries his cock deep inside me with a savage thrust. He rams against the sweetest of sweet spots, which I never knew I had.

I scream. An unintelligible cry of pure bliss that rips from my soul. Spots of color bloom before my eyes, as my entire being tenses, then pulses outward with a force which knocks the breath from my lungs. I spiral, crying out in pleasure as wave after wave of an orgasm like no other washes through me, making me clutch and clench around him, hard.

As if from a distance, I hear him shout, "*Fuck!*"

His hold tightens as he surges within me, his release prolonging my own. I soar high, up to another, more intense peak where the world turns white and all I feel is a delicious rush of super-intense pleasure from the man filling me with his hot, thick seed.

***

Upon opening my eyes, I see him shimmering beside me on the bed. His body seems to literally glow from the thick sheen of sweat which covers him. I blink, and the shimmering recedes to a warm glow cast by the bedside lamp. God in heaven, he's even more gorgeous after sex than before. Resting on his side with his head propped up by his muscular arm. His jaw relaxed, his smile at peace, as he silently watches me. And he still has on that mask. I reach out to touch the tip of his silly Bat Guy ears, but he catches my fingers and brings them to his lips for a warm kiss.

"We're in bed," I state the obvious.

He nods and rubs his thumb across my knuckles, resting our hands on the soft covers, but not letting go. "It seemed the best place to be after you passed out."

"Oh…" I murmur, taken aback. I try to remember what happened after he gave me the best orgasm of my entire life, but my mind blanked out from the overload of pleasure I experienced. I really did pass out. I giggle as I say, "Oh, wow. You must be really pleased."

A glance down the bed reveals my nudity is courteously draped in a soft blanket, while he is gloriously exposed to the lamplight. Looking upwards from his fit legs and semi-hard, magnificently proportioned cock, I catch the concern in his gaze.

"Are you okay?" he asks, his penetrating stare searching my face.

"Yes…no, I… That was…" I swallow hard, trying to find the right words. "That was the most amazing sex I've ever had."

His smile is broad and shows off the perfect line of his gorgeous teeth, but it doesn't seem to reach his eyes.

"Didn't you like it?" I ask, feeling suddenly vulnerable.

"Hell, I liked it too much."

"I know, right? God, when you came it felt like, this…this heat blasted through me. It was like a rush of energy or something."

He grimaces as if my words cause him pain, and his hand slides from my grasp.

"No, no, it was *gooooood*," I insist. "Seriously. I want to do it again. Like now." I quickly grab his hand again and squeeze it, willing him to understand that when I say like now, I mean, *like now*.

But he shakes his head. "I didn't…" His jaw clenches and unclenches as he struggles to explain. "I'm sorry. You're just too hot and sexy. All those little whimpers and moans. I couldn't hold back." Again, that searching gaze. "There may be…repercussions."

"I won't get pregnant, if that's what you mean," I say testily. That hasn't been an option since I was sixteen.

But what if I want to with this man?

The thought sends a shock to my core with its dagger-sharp stab of ridiculousness.

Sarahkka…Sami goddess of childbirth. You remind me of her.

Well, if that's true, I've failed miserably. Ten years ago, despite being an irrational teenager, I wanted that baby with all my heart, but the miscarriage happened anyway. So, I haven't wanted any more. Convinced myself that I'll be happy if I never have any children. Convinced myself it will never happen again, and therefore it never has. But maybe that was a lie. Or worse, an illusion.

What if I actually do have control over these things? It would certainly explain a lot of the oddities in my life.

Like, knowing instinctively when a guy is clean, so I don't have to use a condom. Did that even cross my mind today as an issue? And then there is the fact I'm never wrong about predicting a pregnancy. Not ever. I can feel that tiny heart forming as if it's my own. Christ. Casey is going to go apeshit when I tell her to get ready for having twins.

And now, there's this incredibly sexy man in my life, whose scent is like an arctic forest and who fucks like a wild beast. I can't get enough of him.

"I've never been with a man like you." Letting go of his hand, I stroke his bicep with hesitant fingers, tracing the branches of his antler birthmark. "Not anyone so...beautiful."

Pleasure shoots through me at his easy smile, which this time reaches his eyes.

"I'll tell you what's beautiful." He bends close and touches the tip of my nose with his lips. "This is beautiful." His mouth softly brushes my cheek. "...and this." He moves his lips to hover over mine, pausing briefly in his descent to add, "...and this."

I deepen the kiss immediately, threading my

fingers through his hair as he roughly pulls me over the top of his warm body and clasps me to him.

When we came up for air, I rest my head on his broad chest and feel the steady thud of his heartbeat, so in tune with my own. A nervous laugh slips past my lips. "This is crazy. I feel like I know you. But we haven't met before, have we?" I'm pretty sure I'd remember meeting a guy with his charisma and proportions.

The hours since we met seem to have lengthened into years, each heartbeat a lifetime that is simultaneously forever and gone. A shiver of trepidation creeps through the haze of arousal surrounding me and lodges inside my chest. Things are moving too fast. Before I know it, this night will be done, and my moments with this incredibly sexy man just a memory. A second ago, I wouldn't have cared. But a second is all that realization takes.

His hand strokes my back in a rhythmic soothing motion. I shift to see his face, and his gaze catches mine, grounding me to him. "No, we've never met before," he says. "But I've searched all my life for you."

Damn. I have no doubt he means it because I'm feeling exactly the same way. "Who are you?" A fine growth of stubble tickles my fingers as I stroke his cheek, the heat of his skin a delicious contrast to the cool, leather half-mask that covers his eyes and brow.

"Do you really want to know?"

"No," I whisper as a feeling of foreboding washes through me. "Not yet." Tomorrow will come soon enough. For now, he can be everyman. Any man. My Mystery Lover. For now, he's infallible perfection.

There's no way it can last.

"You're going to break my heart, aren't you?" I abruptly ask.

His gaze never wavers. "Yes, but I have very enjoyable ways of mending it," he says with a smooth smile, but it's shadowed with sadness again.

He looks away and concentrates instead on running his fingers up my thigh. I shiver, my body awakening to him all over again, not that it has ever truly been asleep.

He thinks of me as a goddess, *his* goddess, and he fucks like a freakin' superhero. And, he's hard for me. Thick, long and hard. I'll grasp that while I have it, no matter what hell there might be to pay later.

Something has happened to me tonight, something life-altering and special. No way in hell am I willing to waste it on "what if" fears. Tomorrow can take care of itself.

I answer the hungry question in his eyes with a saucy look of my own. "Just promise me one thing," I say and lightly graze my nails down his ripped abs.

His stomach ripples, flexing the rows of tightly packed muscles beneath. "What's that?"

"This time I get to tie you up and feed you the whipped cream and berries."

The corner of his mouth lifts in a wry grin. "Hold on now," he says. "You don't happen to have some kind of kinky Bat Guy fuck-fetish, do you?"

"Hell, yes," I tease with a laugh, "but only if he's

really you." And wrapping myself around him, I give myself over to his electrifying kiss.

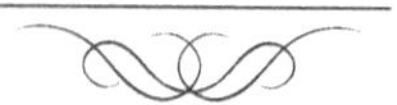

End Notes

Sami: The indigenous inhabitants of Lapland, in the northern most regions of Scandinavia. They have a culture rich in folklore and music, with a deep connection to the land.

Sarahkka: a Sami goddess. She stands as protector of the unborn child and helps the mother give birth. It is she who molds an unborn baby's body around a soul. Traditionally, she sat near the hearth. Drinks were offered to her by women, who also ate a special gruel in her honor. Similar to Artemis/Diana.

Reindeer symbol: In Norway, early huntsmen carved images of reindeer as a symbol of force and power. Reindeer is also the primary herd for the Sami people.

Little Miss
KICK-ASS #2
Secret
Identity
Felicity
Kates

~Astrid~

He's a liar. A manipulator. He doesn't deserve a second chance. But he dominates my dreams, making me want him more each day. My best chance for survival is to stay far away from him. To ignore the desire heating my veins. But trapped together for a cosplay weekend in Sweden, I can't avoid his intoxicating presence…or the way my heart races when he whispers my name.

~Race~

She's the love of my life, my dream, the goddess I've been waiting an eternity for. I won't argue that her anger and mistrust toward me aren't justified, but after nearly thirty days of her constant rebuttal of the obvious fact that she and I belong together, my patience is wearing thin. There is no other option for us. Not when she's the answer to my secret identity.

Our mating under the stars is as inevitable as the sunrise.
Our inherent natures demand it, even if the gods do not.

www.legacyhunter.space

Kate Reedwood also known as Felicity Kates is a Canadian science fiction and romance author, notable for the Amazon bestselling Project Hell series (as Felicity Kates) and the Amazon internationally best-selling Legacy Hunter series, (as Kate Reedwood) co-written with Australian author, Chris Heinicke.

A classically trained writer and artist, with a Bachelor of Arts degree from the University of Guelph as well as a diploma in Classical Animation from world renown, Sheridan College, Kate Reedwood enjoys creating stories that combine humor with strong characters, and adventures which seek to define what it means to be human, no matter the time or place in the universe.

Kate Reedwood lives off coffee (mmmm coffee), enjoys chilling with Netflix shows such as Altered Carbon, and is an avid fan of all things sci-fi, especially Star Wars. When not dreaming up new worlds and books with Chris Heinicke, she can most often be found writing about them

...for reading my books. I hope you have enjoyed them. I love to hear from my readers, so please drop by and leave me a review at the vendor of your choice. You can also email me directly at: **felicitykates.author@gmail.com**

For up to date information on my books, including upcoming releases and giveaways, please visit the KC Stories website at: **www.legacyhunter.space** where you can also sign up for my newsletter and join my Facebook reader group The Legacy Hunter Guild

Science Fiction *Romance* *Suspense*
Urban Fantasy

Find our exciting stories at:
www.Legacyhunter.space

BOOKS BY FELICITY KATES

LITTLE MISS KICK-ASS SERIES
Sizzling contemporary romance with a paranormal twist

Cosplay
Secret Identity

THE NEW EARTH SERIES
Sexually-charged post-apocalyptic sci-fi romance

Project Hell Parts 1-5
Project Hell the complete novel

Books by Chris Heinicke

THE PM SERIES
Thrilling suspense with a sexy dark side.

5 PM
7 PM – Brittany
7 PM – Jack
7 PM – Ed and Hannah
7 PM – Talissa
7 PM – Emily
7 PM – Bjorn
7 PM -- Boxed Set

THE MAN IN BLACK
Out-of-this-world investigative sci-fi

The Man In Black

COMING SOON...THE ZODIAC
SYNDICATE
Urban Fantasy in a MC world
12 book series

BOOKS BY CHRIS HEINICKE AND KATE REEDWOOD

THE LEGACY HUNTER SERIES
Science Fiction Adventure

Queen Killer
Star Keeper
Dark Horizon
Fatal Fortress
Phoenix Rising
Core Shifter (coming soon)
Lost Legacy (coming soon)

COMING SOON…THE GALACTIC MISFITS SERIES
Time travel science fiction adventure set in the Legacy Hunter universe. Featuring Shiznit from the Legacy Hunter series.

Book 1 – *Microscopic Mayhem* available as part of the **UNKNOWN REALMS** anthology.
Buy it now at **www.legacyhunter.space**